ICED IN SHADOW

Immortal Warriors Paranormal Romance

CYNTHIA LUHRS

[faded text]

ADD pht to front...

[faded text] may be reproduced...
medium...
...or permission for the author...
...book review...

1

The dying fire cast ominous shadows across the kitchen walls. Everyone was in bed except the two little brats sneaking cookies. Frederick sneered. It was time to teach the little thieves a lesson they'd never forget.

He'd be damned if he let these little mademoiselles and monsieurs stay in his beloved castle another day. The events of the past year left him crankier than normal. No matter the cost, he was going to be rid of them all before the New Year. Perhaps the next mistress of Ravensmore would be more like his long-dead chatelaine. Someone with ambition and moxie. A mistress he would be proud to serve. Until then, he would bide his time. Alone with his memories.

Giggles brought him back to the scene at hand. The two monsters in question were twins. Four years old and always sneaking cookies from the kitchen after bedtime. This opportunity was too good to pass up. Leaving his perch in the walk-in pantry, the ghost drifted up close to the ceiling in the form of smoke. The siblings pulled a chintz chair over to the counter. The girl clambered up to reach the cookie jar while the boy kept watch.

Waiting until she had her hand in the jar, Frederick changed shape into a horrifying troll-like monster.

"I smell children. Eat children." He lunged for the girl, grabbing the hem of her nightgown while she uselessly kicked, trying to escape. Ice formed and spread midway up the gown, crackling with her every movement.

"Bran help me! It's a monster!" Face white as milk, the little lady screamed and scrambled back. Kicking out, she accidentally knocked the ceramic cookie jar on the stone floor. It shattered on impact, the noise reverberating through the room.

"Children up after bedtime fair game to eat." Frederick lowered his voice to a deep rumble and dragged the girl closer to him. Just as she was close enough for him to see her face, something hit the back of his legs, sending a vibration up his back. Forgetting the girl, he swung around looking for the source. Bran stood facing him, trembling as he held the fireplace poker out in front of him.

"You stay away from my sister, evil troll." The boy's voice shook, his eyes so big they seemed to fill his small face.

"I eat all children in Ravensmore." Grabbing the poker, Frederick pulled the boy close, laying a large, hairy hand on his head. Ice crackled outward, flowing down over the boy, encasing him where he stood. The fire glinted off the icy statue, the expression of shock and horror on the boy's face clear through the ice. Roaring, he turned back to the girl.

She jumped off the counter and ran from the kitchen as fast as her little legs could carry her, screaming the entire way. "Help! There's a monster in the kitchen. Somebody help!"

Footsteps pounded through the castle. Lights clicked on, banishing the darkness. As Colin materialized outside the kitchen, Frederick hid and listened to the conversation.

"Mira, what's the matter? Are ye all right?"

The girl threw herself into Colin's arms. "There's a troll in the kitchen. He was going to eat us. He turned Bran into a statue."

Colin comforted the child as his wife, Emily, appeared along with the butler and cook. They all fussed over the small girl. Once Mira had calmed enough to tell the story, everyone followed her into the kitchen. Wanting to hear the rest without being seen, Frederick turned into a shimmer and hid in a cabinet.

"Look what he did to Bran." Mira ran to her twin touching the ice. A small puddle formed around the base, and the sound of dripping water filled the air.

"Bloody—" Colin stopped.

Him. Frederick sneered. He hated Baron Colin Campbell. Though the look of shock, anger and was that fear from the mighty warrior made it all worthwhile. The Highlander was worried about the brats. Frederick could use this to torture Colin. When Frederick was mortal, the Baron had argued with Abigail, threatened to have Frederick sent back to France. All because of a few complaints from the staff about his high-and-mighty attitude. Why if that Highlander had died and stayed dead like he was supposed to, Frederick wouldn't be in this position now. It was the Baron's fault Frederick was dead.

Why was Colin different from him? While Frederick could pull off a few nasty tricks, Colin was the top of the ghostly food chain. A Shadow Walker.

"Don't worry, lassie. Stand back while I free Bran." Colin walked around the statue, coming to a stop in front of the boy.

Frederick peered out through a crack in the cabinet and watched silver light emanate from Colin's hands, covering his handiwork. Steam filled the room as the ice melted from the frozen statue. Frederick could see the bratty boy blinking and moving his mouth within his icy creation. That would teach the brats to wander around when they should be in bed. Better yet, they should all be locked in their rooms as he was during his childhood in France.

Water ran over the stone floor, and the child collapsed into Emily's outstretched arms.

"Let's get him dried off and some hot chocolate into him." Colin's wife hugged the boy close. "Bran, can you hear me?"

Mira ran to her brother, hugging him tight. Gulping in air like a fish out of water, Bran started crying. "He was so scary. I tried to save Mira. We only wanted some shortbread cookies."

Emily made soothing noises and stroked the boy's hair while the housekeeper brought towels and cleaned up the water.

"Would you check on the rest of the children?" Colin met his butler's gaze.

"Aye, m'lord." The stuffy old guy left the room, and Frederick grimaced. He hated the staff as much as he did the Baron and Baroness Campbell. No more would these people defile Ravensmore. He'd see to it they were all scared off then he could be alone here with his memories of his mistress. And wait.

Knowing he'd soon be found, Frederick vanished to his favorite hiding place at Castle Gloom.

2

"**Y**ou. Give me one good reason I shouldn't blast you to bits." Hamish curled his lip, disgusted to find Frederick hiding in his dungeon.

The traitorous bastard held his hands up in defense. "Please, Lord Hamish. I had to get away from Ravensmore. I didn't know you were back. You're like Colin now. I thought Castle Gloom deserted."

Hamish cocked an eyebrow and let the sarcasm rip. "Really? All the hammering and men running around rebuilding my home didn't clue you in? Maybe I should have put up a sign."

The spiteful being cowered in the last cell in Hamish's dungeon, his shiny black shoes covered in dust, his white tights, ripped. Why the ghost insisted on taking physical form and, even sillier, wearing his ancient French frippery, Hamish didn't have a clue. No matter. First, information, then he'd blast Frederick into oblivion.

Frederick groveled. "I didn't know what Mistress Abigail had planned. It was her idea. I never would have killed the last heir to Ravensmore. You have to believe me."

"Believe you. A French traitor? You hated Ravensmore and all its inhabitants from the day you arrived. Why on earth would you stay behind and haunt the place?" Hamish looked at his watch. The work crew should be arriving soon, and he wanted to go over the next steps. Time to move this along.

"Please, Lord Hamish. Colin wants to send me off to my final rest. I've grown to love Ravensmore, even though it's never been the same without Abigail. It's my duty to stay until another Mistress arrives. One as perfect as Abigail. This current chatelaine, Emily, is a dreadful American." The spirit shuddered and picked at his lace collar.

Before Frederick could react, Hamish shot an energy bolt at him. It nicked the ghost on the leg and the burning smell of electrical wire filled the air. The entity gasped as he faded out to vanish.

"That wasn't fair at all."

"Consider it a warning, servant. I see you on my land again and I'll destroy you for good."

Too bad Hamish wasn't standing closer. Otherwise, he could have grabbed the idiot and sucked the tiny life-force out of him, sending Frederick on to his final rest...and providing Hamish with an energy boost.

Hearing the sound of vehicles approaching, Hamish materialized to the front of the castle.

The man in charge of the project stepped forward. "M'lord, I've drawn up the plans for the next phase. Shall I show you?"

After discussing next steps for his home, Hamish finished the conversation, praising the workmanship. "You and your men are doing good work. The place is starting to look as I remember. I'm sure the other towers and old garrison building will turn out as well. Tell your men not to worry if they hear noises. Gloom isn't haunted, I plan to start spending time here now that two of the towers are habitable."

Bidding the men good day, Hamish went inside one of the completed towers and dematerialized to a seedy area of the Leith Docks known for its illicit offerings. He was hungry. And not for food.

Stalking the inhabitants, Hamish reached out with his senses. By now, Colin should have heard Hamish was back, but as usual either his brother wasn't paying attention to anything that didn't directly impact him or he simply didn't care.

As children, Colin had always been the favorite. His parents doted on their heir while Hamish was largely ignored, treated as the "spare." Anger filling him from old hurts, he caught the faint noise of a commotion taking place down a dark alleyway. The corner of his mouth lifted up in a sneer as he ghosted down the dank, trash-strewn dead-end. The noise of the ships drowned out the sounds. The breeze swept down the alley sending up a swirl of discarded paper and other rubbish. The fresh tang of the water couldn't dispel the stench of the enclosed space around him.

There at the wall, partially hidden by a large trash bin, Hamish spied three men. They had a woman surrounded. He inhaled deeply, taking in the scent of her fear along with another smell of desperation and violence. The woman looked like she'd been on her way home from some banal office job. One of her sensible shoes lay forgotten on the cobblestones. She was dressed in some bland, cheap pants and blazer that did nothing for her.

Another sound propelled Hamish forward. A muffled cry emanated from a clean, worn blue blanket on the ground, now out of reach of the woman. A stroller lay overturned, one wheel still spinning.

"Give us the money now." One of the thugs shook the woman and pushed her up against the wall.

"All I have is twenty quid, take it. Just don't hurt my baby. The ground is much too cold. Let me pick him up." She was sobbing. Mascara ran down her flushed face.

The man went through her bag searching for the money. Pawing through the belongings, he threw a baby bottle full of milk to the ground where it rolled under a trash bin. Disgust filled the man's face as he tossed the worn diaper bag over his shoulder.

"Well lads, since this fine lady doesn't have anything else of value, let's have a bit o' fun with her. Me first." The man back-handed the woman and nodded to his compatriots to hold her while he fumbled for the zipper underneath his ponderous belly. The woman's frantic screams were drowned out by the horn of a large freighter coming into port.

An innocent woman. Working a menial job in a bad part of town, trying to make a living and take care of her babe. Rage filled Hamish. He'd had his fair share of women, but he'd never forced a woman. Thinking back on the scullery girl of his youth, his vision turned black. He'd bedded the lass and later when she came to him and told him she was with child, he panicked. Afraid of his father's ire, Hamish went to meet her at the River of Sorrow at Castle Gloom. He planned to pay her off and send the chit away.

When he arrived she was dead. Must have gotten too close to the edge, fell in, and drowned. She couldn't swim. Instead of telling anyone, he ran away and pretended nothing was wrong. Acted surprised when he learned of her death. When his father asked him if he had anything to do with the girl's demise, Hamish swore he didn't, and the matter went away.

Part of him wondered if that's why he was in some kind of limbo all those centuries.

He'd deserved the punishment for not making things right.

Not only with the girl but also with his brother. If he was honest Hamish didn't expect Colin to ever forgive him.

Could he ever find a way to forgive himself? To make the best of this second chance?

Given another go at life, Hamish had vowed never again to turn away from an innocent woman.

The second man slugged the woman. Once in the stomach and again in the face. She crumpled to the ground, silent. "That'll shut her trap."

It happened so quickly, the thugs barely had time to process what was happening. Hamish materialized out of the light fog rolling in, grabbing the ringleader with his pants halfway undone, lifting him off the ground with ease. The man let out a grunt of surprise.

"Preying on a mother. One trying to feed her babe. The lot of you should be ashamed." Hamish assessed every potential weapon from the rusted piece of metal leaning against the trash bin to the broken bottles littering the cobblestones.

"Look man, we found her first so she's ours." Man number two spoke up.

The third loser chimed in, "Back the hell off, and go get your own slag."

Tsking, Hamish raked a glare over the three men. The third man stank of disease. While he couldn't catch anything, the illness would leave a sour, sick taste in the man's life-force. Shooting a bolt of sizzling power, it arced and hit the man in the chest. He fell to the ground unmoving. The authorities would assume he'd been struck by lightning.

"What the fuck was that shit?" The first man furiously kicked and tried to pry Hamish's hands from his neck while Hamish held him a good six inches off the ground.

Not bothering to answer, he sent a tendril of energy out, effectively wrapping the man he was holding in vines of electricity. Dropping him to the ground, Hamish kicked him in the ribs. "Stay put while I take care of your mate."

The second man held the baby by its faded blue blanket. "Come any closer, and I'll throw it to the ground."

A broken laugh escaped from Hamish. This pathetic excuse for a human thought he could get the drop on him? Throwing his hand out, a bubble of green and purple luminescence encircled the child, holding the small boy aloft. The second man gaped stupidly at the sight.

"What, a lightning bolt to your mate's heart didn't surprise you but this does? By the gods, humans haven't evolved at all.

You're dumber than the humans in my day." The man kept blinking at the sight of the baby floating in the air, his face pale as the fog thickened, swirling through the alley, obscuring the ground.

Hamish was done playing. Two steps terminated the distance between them. He reached out, pulling the man close. The air changed, the scent of an electrical storm filled the rank alley as Hamish fed. Holding his hands to either side of the man's face, he inhaled deeply.

Faint brown and gray mist seemed to seep out of the man's nose, eyes, and mouth into Hamish. The man's life-force had the taint of a heavy drug user The taste rancid on his tongue. Dirty, matted black hair turned white, the face sunk in on itself like a balloon left alone to deflate. Grimacing at the taste, Hamish pulled harder and felt the man's heart flutter twice and then stop. The man looked confused as he died, wondering what was happening.

Dropping the discarded shell to the ground, Hamish threw his head back enjoying the sensation of energy flowing through him, boosting his power. With a glance at the trussed-up man, Hamish smiled. "Your turn."

Wiping a hand across his mouth, Hamish felt as if he could rule the world. Power coursed through him, and in that moment, he could understand why his enemy fed on humans. Technically, he and his brethren were forbidden from stealing energy from humans. Though Hamish figured lowlife scum weren't included in that mandate. A whimper brought his attention back to the situation at hand.

Taking hold of the babe, he released the energy holding the child aloft. The tiny boy gazed up at Hamish with trusting eyes, sending a fission of pain through his gut. How many times had he looked to his parents for love and affection only to be pushed aside for his perfect brother? Recoiling as the infant reached a small fist out, Hamish knelt by the mother.

The woman was out cold. Hamish gathered her belongings,

wiping off the bottle he fished out from under the trash bin. Placing the wallet back in the bag, he paused, reached in his pocket and added a handful of bills. Hamish laid the babe in the mother's lap along with the battered bag and shoe before he changed forms. He didn't want to speak to her, pretend to be something he wasn't.

The fog would cover the bodies, and the authorities would add these to the growing tally of unsolved murders for the year. Looking around, Hamish realized life in modern-day Scotland wasn't so very different from his own time—well as far as the preying upon the weak, murder and mayhem. The technological advances would have been considered witchcraft in his time.

Coming to, the woman whimpered when she touched the cut on her lip. Opening her eyes, she cried out seeing the babe safe.

Hamish hovered above her, invisible. She patted the child, unwrapped the dingy blanket and checked him over. Hamish listened to her sobbing. "Thank you God for protecting my baby." He resisted the urge to roll his eyes. God played no part in today's events. Instead her prayer was answered by a damaged man who wasn't sure what he believed anymore.

❧ 3 ❧

I ce coated the hallway outside the bedchamber. Frozen fingers spread out as if seeking the darkness, creating a pattern that looked rather like an inkblot on the stone. The shadows from the hall lights trapped within the glistening crystals. Colin frowned. *What the hell?* Opening the door, he caught sight of a man in a dark green velvet coat with lace dripping from the sleeves. As he watched, the man disappeared into the wall.

Blasted Frederick. He'd had enough of the spirit's antics. A scowl worked its way across his face, and he shook his head.

"What the bloody hell happened in here?" Colin bellowed at the empty room.

Emily was fuming over the ghost terrorizing the children. This latest incident would be one more strike against the spirit. Before him, the wardrobe doors gaped open. One swinging haphazardly from its broken hinge. His wife's clothing lay scattered across the room, ripped to shreds.

The floor, wardrobe, and remnants of fabric were all coated in ice. It was the last straw. The wretch loved to frighten the children, popping up in the middle of their beds, holding his head under his arm floating around the room moaning. Colin couldn't count the number of times he'd woken to find three or four little ones in bed with he and Emily or curled up in front of the fire, bundled up in blankets like a pile of sleepy puppies.

Frederick claimed he still watched over the ladies of Ravensmore, but caused trouble was more like it. Last year when Colin met Emily, the ghost spun ugly lies, causing her to run away. Colin held him partly responsible for her subsequent capture and torture.

Since she'd come into his life, time seemed to pass quickly. They'd already been married a little over a year and Colin wanted to drop to his knees and thank the goddess Terya each and every day for bringing them together. For giving them the twins.

Spiteful Frederick had been hiding from Colin for a year. Truth be told he'd been a bit busy to worry about taking care of the issue, but now...things had gone too far. Today was December twenty-first, the Winter Solstice—Colin's Shadow Walker powers were enhanced during each solstice as were all Shadow Walkers. Time to rid Ravensmore of this nuisance once and for all.

"What on earth happened in here?" Emily stepped into their bedroom and knelt down. Holding up a sodding pile of rags, she fumed. "I hate that horrible little man. Ever since he tried to turn me against you last year, he's been nothing but pure trouble." She kicked the tatters that recently were her clothes.

"That vindictive little rat needs to go." Dropping the wet mess, a look of supreme distaste on her face, she stood, gray eyes flashing like a winter thunderstorm, her cheeks red as rubies. "Enough."

Leaning down to kiss his American wife, Colin fisted his hands in her long brown hair and inhaled.

"Well, that's one way to take my mind off this mess. But you can't go around kissing me day and night."

"I don't know why not. Sounds like a perfectly good way to spend the long winter days." He leered at his beautiful wife.

She'd blessed him with two perfect twins. He swore he loved them more with every day that passed.

Emily rolled her eyes. "It's almost Christmas. I won't have anything to wear."

"Never fear, lass. Easy enough to procure new clothes for you. Don't worry. I'll take care of Frederick."

"Good. I'll cheer when that beastly creature is gone. Turning into a troll to scare the children. It's reprehensible."

After sending word to have the room cleaned, Colin went searching for the nasty spirit. Changing into his natural form of pure energy, he checked all the usual haunts, favorite places of Abigail, but there was no sign of the traitor. Frederick was a wily little bastard. Seemed to have a nose for knowing when Colin was on the warpath and vanished for a few days.

Cursing, Colin re-formed to his human guise and was startled when a small voice spoke to him.

"M'lord Colin? There's a man who talks funny and has on silly clothes hiding in my wardrobe. And my room's all covered in ice, like outside when it snows."

Emily always wanted a big family so last year they'd decided to take in lost children. Ravensmore Castle was large with plenty of room. It was the least they could do for these casualties of the Walker War. At last count they had thirty-one kids living with them. Some days it was hard to keep track of them all. The boy looked to be four or five. He'd been with them for six months now. What was the lad's name again? Colin wracked his brain. "Silly clothes?"

"Like the people in the pictures on the walls." The lad pointed to ancient family portraits hanging in the hallway.

Taken down by a child. Made Colin want to roar with laughter. It was fascinating to him that small children seemed to be able to see them all. But once they hit about six or seven the ability wore off. Or more likely, the kids stopped believing in fantastical tales, and once they stopped believing, they stopped seeing.

"Mingus, excellent work. Which room is yours?"

"The one with the Celtic poster on the door. Last night the ghost turned into giant snakes in the shower. Then he hid under my bed, grabbed my ankle when I got in." Mingus shivered. "He's verra scary."

"Dinna fash yourself, lad. I'll take care of him; he'll no longer be a problem. The snakes aren't real, it's illusion—like on the telly." Ruffling the boy's hair, Colin sent him on his way. "Now go on to the kitchen and ask Cook for a cinnamon roll." Mingus ran out of the room grinning from ear to ear.

Colin dematerialized into the boy's room. Many of the rooms didn't have closets so the children used huge wardrobes to store their belongings. Antiques, not that the kids cared. He wasn't giving Frederick another chance to escape. Colin raised both hands, shooting blue and silver energy in the form of an iridescent net into the wardrobe. A startled cry rang out as he reeled out the catch.

"Damnation." Nice, he'd captured a shoe with an ornate buckle. The sneaky troublemaker had gotten away. Flinging the wardrobe door wide, he saw the problem. A mirror was leaning against the back effectively blocking the net. Powers were great except when thwarted by something as ordinary as a blasted piece of glass.

Now the spirit had been warned and would be that much more difficult to catch. Standing, thinking of options, Colin decided to enlist Robert's help to stop Frederick from terrorizing those under his protection. They'd snare the bastard on Christmas Eve. Would be a perfect gift for Emily.

❧ 4 ☙

The weather was unseasonably warm considering it was December. Though to Emily, born and bred in Charleston, South Carolina, it was still freaking cold. The twins, Colleen and Naill, were almost six months old and antsy. The winter sun shining, she bundled them up, put them in the waiting sleigh, greeting the horses. Whispering and patting the two black horses, she produced an apple for each from her coat pocket and set out for a ride around the grounds.

Leaving the castle, Emily urged the horses into a brisk trot, smiling at the twins tucked into the cozy blankets in the sleigh. The cold air smelling of forest and earth made her feel alive.

She and Colin were starting a tradition. Inviting trusted friends and other Shadow Walkers to spend the holiday at Ravensmore. Emily's parents were killed in a boating accident when she was in college. It had been a hard year. Kendrick's murder, hearing horrors on the news and knowing the enemy was to blame. Losing the ones you loved tended to put life into perspective.

Spooked, the horses stopped, tossing their heads. The skies darkened and fast-moving clouds blotted out the sun. Had a Day Walker come to harm her babies? Emily looked around, but they were all alone. Nothing but desolate countryside as far as the eye could see.

Putting her hand on the edge of the sleigh, she jerked it back. Ice crawled up the brightly colored exterior and over the sides, freezing her in place. Helpless, she watched the strange dark-colored ice cover her children while she was unable to save them. It was as if everything was iced in shadow.

The babies weren't moving. Encased in ice, pale and lifeless, they lay still. The world turned gray, and Emily fought to hold on as she forced every ounce of energy into breaking free. Fingers twitched, and a faint crack sounded, loud as a firecracker in the silence.

Sending out a plea to the goddess Terya who'd helped her save Colin last year, Emily smelled gardenias. Taking it as a sign she wiggled her fingers feeling the ice shift. Able to move, she slammed her hands outward against the ice. The cracking noises filled the air, and the ice started dripping, melting away as fast as it had covered her and the children.

Pulling her foot loose, she freed herself and lunged for the children. Naill was moving, whimpering from the cold and wet. Colleen was blue. Emily screamed as if her very soul was shattering. Patting her daughter, she leaned close, something shifted, the shadows dissipated, the pale sunlight returned, and her gurgling baby was back. Birds chirped, and a breeze ruffled her hair. Both babies were fine.

Colin materialized in front of her. "Gods, lass! My heart is beating out of my chest. Are you harmed?"

Last year Emily and Colin had sacrificed all for each other. She remembered Terya's words, *if one of you is killed, the other will die at the same time, as you share one heart.* Colin could feel the pain in her heart as could she his.

"The babies were encased in ice." Emily stopped, willed herself to calm and told Colin the rest.

He stiffened. Bending down, he examined the remnants of ice still encrusted on the frame and wheels of the carriage.

"What the bloody hell is Frederick playing at?" The tic in Colin's jaw twitched to the beat of her heart. "He's always played harmless pranks, but ever since the twins were born it's gotten worse. He's become a danger to us all."

Anger welled up inside Emily. "This has to stop. You have to do something to get rid of him. It was bad enough I was walled up in the dungeon because of him but to harm the children? I won't have it."

"I'll take care of him, love."

Emily scowled at her husband. She loved him beyond measure, but right now she could spit nails. "You've been saying that over and over. See that you do, or you'll be sleeping alone until he's gone."

Her husband knew better than to make a remark or even crack a smile. "Why don't you and the babies come back with me? I'll have one of the lads fetch the sleigh and horses."

"That low-life jerk isn't ruining my day. We're going to finish our ride, and then I'll be back."

Colin stood watching her with a scowl on his face.

"Really. I need a bit of time to calm down anyway before I come back to make cookies with Meg and the kids. We'll be fine."

Kissing her on the cheek, he said, "If you're sure?" Emily arched an eyebrow. With a grim look, Colin dematerialized to hunt the French bastard down.

The only sign anything had happened was a wet puddle on the ground. Checking her children once more, satisfied they were okay, Emily climbed into the carriage seat. Not even a foul-tempered spirit was going to ruin her mood. Emily urged the horses on.

Over the past year she'd become adept at riding and handling horses. The twins adored the big beasts, reaching out tiny hands to pat the animals and blowing bubbles when one of the horses nuzzled them.

Christmas was almost here. The time had passed so quickly.

ICED IN SHADOW

Finding Colin, getting married, and then the twins. Life was perfect. The horses were happy, trotting along, bells lightly jangling.

Breathing easier, relaxing, she thought about the next few days. Everyone was coming to Ravensmore for Christmas Eve dinner.

Monroe arrived that morning. Last year, Emily met Monroe when he was still a cop. On vacation in Scotland, she and her best friend Kat returned one day to find their hotel room had been ransacked. Monroe and his partner showed up to investigate. After finding out the world wasn't what it seemed, he ended up losing his job and started his own business as a private investigator.

Tomorrow afternoon would bring Robert and Maggie. Robert was a Shadow Walker like Colin, and Emily adored the pirate. It had been quite a shock when Robert called to say he was getting married. Emily swore he'd be a playboy for eternity. Funny how meeting your soul mate changed everything.

Then there would be all the children Robert and Maggie had taken in at Robert's home, Gwrych Castle. There were twenty-five living at the castle. Given Robert couldn't stand kids, Emily wondered how he was adjusting to the upheaval in his normally child-free life.

With over fifty children at Ravensmore for Christmas Eve, it would be noisy. Emily's heart seized thinking of those children still out there, alone and unwanted, lost to the streets. Exploited by the enemy.

And let's not forget Draken and Fury. Draken was a dragon and Fury a huge hound with three heads. The kids loved them both, no fear at all. Adults knew better.

Castle Gloom appeared in front of her. She'd been so lost in thinking about the guests arrival, she'd gone further than planned. Odd, there was work going on. Did Colin say he was rebuilding? With the twins and children running around it was

19

no wonder she forgot things. Curiosity got the better of her, and Emily urged the horses closer for a look.

A couple of the towers had been rebuilt. Men were everywhere, scurrying here and there, shouting orders. Urging each other to finish up and leave for the long holiday weekend. Some had already started packing up, leaving as she made her way through the construction.

There was Colin, standing near the old garrison building. She'd thought he was going back to Ravensmore to hunt for Frederick.

"Colin." Emily called out, waving, the bells on the sleigh announcing her arrival. "I didn't know you'd started work on the castle. I probably forgot. I'd forget my head if it wasn't attached to my body."

Her husband turned around.

Only it wasn't him.

❧ 5 ❧

Frederick turned to mist and hid behind the tapestry in the great hall. It was the perfect place to spy on everyone.

Three children ran into the room, and Frederick blew a gust of wind knocking them over like tumbleweeds as they rolled through the hall, striking the huge dining table. The kids cried out in pain while Frederick resisted the urge to snicker and give away his hiding place.

He remembered when the tapestry was hung. So long ago.

Abigail, may she rest in peace, brought Frederick to this castle in the wilds of Scotland. He'd been nothing more than a common thief, not a very good one either. She found him lying in a gutter after a group of Scottish nobles left him beaten and bloody for helping himself to a few baubles and quid in a tavern. After cleaning him up and admiring the beautiful ring he'd filched, she offered him a position at the castle.

The staff was offended the mistress of Ravensmore Castle would have a Frenchman serve her. Every day they found a new way to mistreat him, humiliate him. Each day brought another terrible torment.

Abigail alone protected him, elevated him to be her personal manservant. Provided him with proper clothes. Promised he would have a home with her always. Engaged to marry Baron Colin Campbell, she plotted with his younger brother to kill the Highlander. Once the deed was done Abigail married Hamish. After sufficient time had passed, she schemed to have Hamish murdered as well. In Frederick's estimation, she was a fine lady with an eye for advancement. Dreadful how Colin's nasty friend Robert had taken revenge. Frederick sniffed and twisted his brown shoulder-length hair into a knot. A terrible shame in his opinion. The pirate shipped Abigail off to work as a maid for a plantation owner in the Caribbean.

In mourning for his beloved mistress, he wasn't paying attention, and one morning so many years ago, sitting in the open window, Colin appeared out of the wall to stand in front of him. It startled Frederick so badly he fell backwards out of the opening, breaking his neck in the fall.

Drifting out from behind the tapestry, Frederick rolled his eyes. The staff was talking about his latest escapades.

"The Baron will rid us of this nuisance." The housekeeper shook her head, sending hairpins flying across the room.

The crotchety old butler spoke in a low voice, "Don't worry. By the new year we'll have peace and quiet...well as much as we can with all the little ones running around."

Sniffing, Frederick manifested big black rats and sent them scurrying across the hall. Gratified to hear the expletives and shrieking, he vanished to hide in one of the unused rooms, shoulders shaking with laughter.

Baron Campbell. Frederick detested the Shadow Walker. Of course Colin would fight for the good guys. Over the years, he'd seen Colin battle his enemy, the Day Walkers. Somehow these men were given another try at life. Swearing to protect or destroy humanity depending on which side they fought for.

Why wasn't Frederick offered the same chance for advancement?

All who refused to move on to the final realm, remaining

behind, kept their soul. The soul, Frederick learned, was the energy life-force within. That Colin was so powerful made Frederick despise him all the more.

Over the years the castle became Frederick's second chance, his sanctuary after Abigail was gone... For almost four hundred years, he waited for another mistress, one deserving of Ravensmore.

The American, Emily, would have to go.

Wow! Hamish was the spitting image of Colin. Looking closer Emily detected slight differences. The man stood on the wall like he owned it. He was shorter than Colin by a good four or five inches, and his build wasn't as muscular. Though they had the same chestnut hair and green eyes. This man had short hair where Colin's was long. They could easily pass for brothers.

"I'm sorry...I thought you were someone else."

Who was he? The man jumped down from a partially built wall and stalked over to her.

"You must be Emily. We haven't had the pleasure, though I'm sure you've heard all about me."

The man cocked his head at her. Was he some long-lost relative? "I'd remember if we'd met. Forgive me, but who are you?"

Choked laughter rang out on the cold air, startling the ravens perched in a nearby tree. The birds took flight, cawing their displeasure.

"Oy! Lord Campbell. Me and the boys are finished for the day. We'd best get home before our missus have our heads." A man in rough workman's clothing tipped his hat to the man in front of her.

Lord Campbell?

The only other man with that title died hundreds of years ago ... it couldn't be. Was he some kind of scam artist?

The Colin look-alike inclined his head in a gesture Emily knew very well. Her gasp caused him to turn and stare at her for a long moment before he answered the workman.

"Good work today. You'll find a bottle of Ravensmore whisky for each of the men."

The workman grinned. "We'll be enjoyin' it tonight."

With that, he called to his crew to pack it in.

Emily watched the workman tidy up the area. Vehicles started to leave the castle. Her breathing quickened, and she cleared her throat, swallowing. This man had to be a relation of Colin's. The two of them stood alone. Facing each other. The air stilled, and the castle held its breath, waiting. Emily's breath snaked out in an icy cloud as the temperature dropped. Worried about the twins, she darted a glance to the sleigh to make sure her children were still bundled under the warm, wool blankets. Both were sound asleep. Moving in front of the sleigh, Emily put herself between them and him. Unease wound its way around her neck, frozen fingers cutting off her air supply. She'd learned to trust her instincts and every one told her the man in front of her was a lion waiting to pounce.

"Who am I? I'm rather wounded you don't know. Why I am your dear brother-in-law, Hamish." The man bowed, his words sharp as a knife.

"Hamish. But you died in 1646. How is that possible?"

Colin's brother was here? What had happened? She was damn sure Colin didn't know. After all, this was the man who betrayed and murdered her husband. If Colin knew Hamish had returned Emily would have heard about it. Every instinct screamed at her to protect the children. To run.

The babies woke, gurgling, warm in the sleigh. Hamish moved closer for a look. Cautiously, Emily stood next to him, poised to jump in and take off. Energy coursed through her veins, itching, wanting to escape. Reeling from the news, she wondered—was he a Shadow Walker too? Or even worse, was he a Day Walker?

Oblivious to her distress, he continued. "'Tis a boring story. But rest assured, 'tis me. Thorne brought me back." Hamish looked into the sleigh. "Babies. Horrible little things."

Thorne was the god of Shadows. It was he, in the darkness of the Shadow realm, who offered the choice to become a Shadow Walker. A small measure of calm bubbled up at hearing Thorne's name. Swallowing, she realized Colin's brother was back from the dead—as one of the good guys.

Lord have mercy, Colin was going to hit the roof when he found out.

Back to the matter at hand. Act nice, and he'll be nice. Show fear, and all is lost. Summoning strength from deep within, she sent a plea up to Terya and acted. Enveloping Hamish in a hug, Emily wasn't surprised when he jerked out of her reach.

"Never do that again if you want to live."

She gave him her most charming Southern smile. Emily learned at an early age when dealing with troublemakers or in an unsafe situation to act like everything was normal. Hamish might not know she knew his history. Knew the treachery he'd committed. So she pretended as an idea formed in her mind.

"Hamish. Colin's younger brother. It's so nice to meet you. Sorry I hugged you. It's just...you're Colin's only living family and that makes you my family too." Pausing, she watched the angry confused look on his face. "The past is the past. Have you been... back...long?" Obviously this wasn't what he expected from her. Picking up her son, she showed him to Hamish while keeping a firm hold on her boy. "This is Naill. He and Colleen are almost six months old."

He backed up as if he were afraid of the babies. "Where's Colin?" Looking around, his eyes probed every stone and pile of rubble around the castle as if her husband would jump out any second and scream boo.

"He's at the house. We're getting ready for Christmas. Does Colin know you're going to be ... um, working together?"

It was so disconcerting looking at him, seeing her wonderful husband's face staring back at her. Hamish's face had an angry set to it. Harsh lines around the mouth and eyes. A cold, dead look in his eyes.

Barking out a sound halfway between a laugh and a cough, he sneered at her. "No, and if you know what's good for you, you won't say a word. I'll visit my dear brother to make my presence known in my own sweet time."

Emily knew with every fiber of her being that Colin and his brother were sworn enemies. Yet, after losing her parents years ago, Emily's perspective had drastically shifted. She believed deep within her soul everyone needed family.

And despite knowing the heinous act Hamish had committed against Colin, she had to believe with enough time they could start again. Heck, they were immortal; they had eternity to fix this. Her husband had changed; his hatred didn't burn as bright, so she wondered, could Colin and Hamish find the path to reconnect? To forgive and begin again? Just because Emily wanted a reconciliation, it didn't mean she trusted Hamish as far as she could throw him. He'd have to be watched. To prove himself worthy of forgiveness.

Wasn't Christmas the ideal time to start anew? There would be other Shadow Walkers there to watch out for trouble. And they were on the same side now.

Maybe Hamish had changed too?

Being an orphan, she knew how important family was, having that one person in the world to always be there for you. Emily sent up a Christmas wish to Terya.

Taking a deep breath, she let it out slowly, carefully choosing the words. "Please come to Ravensmore for Christmas Eve dinner. Everyone will be there. You're family—you should be there. Talk to Colin. Make amends."

He looked at her like she was crazier than her Aunt LouAnne

before dematerializing, leaving her stunned and shaking.

❧ 7 ❧

O ver at Gwrych Castle, a knock at his study door had Robert looking up from the latest shipping reports. A small girl of four stood there, uncertain, biting her lip. "Mr. Robert, can I come in?"

With a home rapidly filling with kids, Robert didn't have to expand the tiny amount of energy to make himself constantly visible. Young children with open hearts could see Shadow Walkers and other beings whether or not they willed it. All the youngsters quickly accepted his disappearances and his other unusual guests as a normal part of their new lives.

What was the chit's name? "Ah, Melody. What can I do for you?" With boys it was easy; he put them into training with sword and dagger or they wanted to learn how to sail and worked on one of his ships. But girls... He wasn't sure what to do with them.

Maggie laughed, her green eyes flashing, and said, ask them. Told him they might want to learn to use a sword or sail.

Times had changed, for the better in his mind.

Since that conversation, he was careful to tell the children they could do whatever they wanted. Told them all the options instead of one for the boys and another for the girls. He was still getting used to having the little monsters running around. They'd overrun Gwrych, turned his household upside down. And the mess! He'd never seen such disorder. Now he had a staff devoted to taking care of things. Everyone else was happy, but he was reserving judgment for now.

The girl had big blue eyes and pale blonde hair. She approached him as if he was some kind of wild animal and she wasn't sure if he'd eat her or not. Leaning back in his chair, he waited to see what she wanted so badly she'd venture into his domain. All the other children avoided the study at all costs. Of course, this was where they were sent if they'd been naughty, so it probably held all kinds of bad connotations in their little minds. They weren't spanked. That was useless. Instead he figured out what mattered most to them and took it away. If a child loved to read, then their punishment was no books for a number of days or weeks depending on the seriousness of the infraction.

"Tommy said we could do whatever we wished with the Christmas money you and Mrs. Maggie gave us. Is that true? *Anything* we want?"

"Aye." What did she want? Sweets or new clothes? Each child had been given one hundred quid to do with as they wished for the holiday. Unbeknownst to the kids, they'd receive presents from Santa and much-needed clothing from everyone at Gwrych on Christmas morning. He'd already set aside a trust for each child to ensure they could go to university or start a business, whatever they wanted to do with their lives. Enough to begin a new life when the time came. Of course, that assumed there'd still be a world where university was important. Given the state of things he wasn't sure how things would look in the next ten or fifteen years. But he was sure they'd need money. There was always a need for gold. Some things never changed.

Standing up straight, she marched right up to the edge of his desk, clambered up in the chair, stood and looked him in the eye.

A serious look on her elfin face. He resisted the urge to laugh—just barely.

"I don't need the money and I have a home here so I want to give my money to help the animals. The ones with no home or food. Can you help me do that?"

He was dumbfounded.

Undaunted, Melody continued. "And if I could have a kitty for my own, I would like that a lot. I asked Santa instead of bringing me presents, to find homes for all the unwanted animals but I forgot to tell him I would very much like a baby cat for myself."

Just when he'd convinced himself the kids were nothing but a nuisance, this one had to go and cock it all up. Had to clear his throat before he answered. "That is a splendid idea. And yes, you may have a kitten of your own." He thought a moment and later would wonder whatever possessed him to such madness. "Melody, how would you like to help me start a home for animals here at Gwrych? We have the barn and stables and there are a few other buildings we can put to good use. It would mean a great deal of hard work. Do ye think you're up to it?"

Before he could move, the chit closed the small distance separating them, clambering across the desk, scattering papers to the floor and threw her arms around his neck.

"Oh, thank you, Mr. Robert. I love you." Kissing him on the cheek, she scampered out of the study, skipping and singing softly to herself.

What had he gotten himself into now? Sighing, he called his steward in and apprised him of the latest development. To his credit the man didn't say a word other than the corner of his mouth turning up, he simply started making arrangements.

Later that night at dinner, he told Maggie about Melody and her selfless request. Suppressing a laugh, Maggie's eyes shone. "You're such a big softie. From the guy who couldn't stand little ankle biters to now having an animal sanctuary in addition to a home and school for children...I love you very much."

"Don't let it get around. I have a reputation to uphold. I'll make smugglers out of the lot of 'em."

Finishing dinner, they went to the great hall to check on the children. Sometimes they ate with the kids, other times Robert and Maggie preferred to eat alone in the small dining room, thankful for a break from the chaos and noise. Standing in the room, it quieted quickly when the children noticed Robert. They told stories about him, and many were both in awe and fear of him in equal measure. 'Twas good for keeping order.

"Melody, come up here." The little girl bounded up, pigtails flying, and took his hand in her tiny palm. She carried a dingy white stuffed cat in her other hand. He knelt. "Would you like to tell everyone our plan?"

Eyes shining, Melody told the others what she planned to do. She finished with, "And I'm giving my hundred quid to help start things. We're going to need lots of helpers to take care of and feed the animals. Would any of you like to help?"

Hand after hand rose in the air. Voices rang out. "I want to give my money to the animals too."

"Can we get a horse?"

"I want to take care of the dogs."

On and on it went. Maggie wiped a tear away. Robert raised a hand, bringing the room back to order. "You are all verra kind-hearted. Animals need our help too. Write out a list of what kinds of animals you'd like to care for." He turned to go. "Keep your money, kids. This one's on Maggie and me. An early Christmas present."

Shouts filled the room as they swarmed him. Fear forgotten, they hugged him and Maggie. There was much chattering away to each other.

"I hope none of them ask for a lion or tiger." Robert wasn't sure what he'd find on the list.

Maggie laughed and kissed him. "As much as you love treasure, I'm shocked you'd part with any of it."

"Hrmph. Don't tell anyone, but the munchkins have grown

on me. Anyway, we've rooms full of treasure after relieving the old Knights Templar of what they'd left behind, forgotten for centuries. Not like they needed it anymore."

"Good thing. I hear Chester saying he wants elephants. Might want to look into acquiring some more land around the castle..."

"Bloody hell. I should have said normal animals. You know cats, dogs, rabbits, hamsters, hedgehogs...regular pets. No lions, tigers, or bloody elephants."

Smiling, they went upstairs to bed.

Maggie stepped out of the bathroom and stopped. There in the center of the room was a large box wrapped in festive paper —birthday paper.

"What's this? Did you run out of Christmas paper?" she teased him, running a hand along the ribbon on the box.

"You neglected to tell me it was your birthday in November. So we're celebrating now."

Standing in the room, shirtless, lit by the fire, Robert looked like the cover of a magazine for sexiest man alive with his jet-black hair and indigo eyes. Especially when he smiled. He was her best friend. Her lover. Her other half.

"Well, go on then, open it." He urged her, eyes shining.

"I've never had a birthday celebration or a present." Tearing into the pink and white paper with abandon, she lifted the lid off the box. Pulling away light pink tissue paper revealed a smaller box. Within the box were three pictures. The first was of a greenhouse like the ones here at Gwrych. The second image was of cranberries, and the third photo showed a pile of books. Looking at Robert with wide eyes, she started to sniffle.

"Given your fondness for sugared cranberries, I thought you might like a building full of them. I talked to a master gardener who assured me the berries could be grown as trailing plants in hanging baskets or in a sunken bed. Don't worry, I ordered a huge industrial freezer, though I'm guessing the munchkins will adore the berries too. The workers will start building the green-house next week."

"It's wonderful. I can't wait to have my very own cran-berries."

She ran her fingers over the picture of the books. Chuckling, Robert solved the mystery for her. "Since I didn't know what you like to read, I ordered you a bit of everything. Shall we go see?"

Eyes wide, she jumped up. "Do you have to ask?"

They dematerialized and Robert told her to close her eyes. "No peeking." Maggie nodded. "Remember the empty room next to your solar?" Another nod. "Now it is m'lady's own library. Open your eyes, love."

Books. Everywhere. From floor to ceiling. The room had a beautiful Persian rug along with comfy-looking sofas and chairs scattered around. Tables had been placed next to each seating area, topped with antique lamps casting a warm glow over the room. A fire crackled in the fireplace. Dark wood bookcases lined the room, with a rolling ladder to get to the ceiling that must have been twenty feet high. "I could read forever and never read them all."

Before she could utter another word, the doors flew open and children streamed in singing Happy Birthday. Their tiny voices mixed with the deeper voices of Robert's crew, who were gathered at one end of the room. Four children pushed a rolling cart into the room with the biggest cake she'd ever laid eyes on. It was pink with red, purple and white flowers all over. Candles burned, and the kids yelled. "Make a wish and blow them out!"

Obliging, Maggie closed her eyes and wished for many more perfect moments exactly like this one. In one big breath she blew them all out. Cheering ensued. The cake alternated layers of chocolate, strawberry, and yellow. There were real flowers as well, violets dipped in sugar, decorating the confection.

Robert's crew came forward. The young man, Ian handed her an envelope. "From all of us, m'lady. Happy birthday."

Opening the envelope, Maggie gasped. It was a picture of

carved wooden doors. The carvings were of all kinds of fruits and vegetables. She looked at all of them, words failing her.

Ian grinned. "We all took turns with the carving. Thought it could be for your new greenhouse." He blushed as Maggie threw her arms around him.

"I don't know what to say. It's a work of art. I shall treasure it always and smile every morning when I open the doors."

There was good-natured grumbling from the crew, and someone called out, "Don't hog the lady, Ian. We all want a hug."

Robert laughed. "Easy with my lady. Now, who wants cake?" A chorus of "me, me" filled the room. "Alright then. Line up and I'll do the honors."

The kids ran to the front of the line, waiting their turn. He handed a piece to Maggie and watched her take a bite.

"This is delicious. I think I'll have another piece before the little angels eat it all."

He smiled and placed a second slice on the plate.

Draken wriggled into the room. Robert still couldn't believe a bloody dragon followed them home from Rosslyn Chapel. Draken had retracted the spikes on his tail and tucked his great leathery wings close to his body so he wouldn't break any of the furniture. The light in the room hit his iridescent scales, casting a rainbow of colors on the walls.

"I lit the candles myself. Happy birthday, Maggie." The dragon turned a gold eye on Robert. "Sugar for the kiddies before bed... You have a great deal to learn."

Robert chuckled and motioned to his crew, who were fighting over who had the biggest flowers on their piece. "They'll be worse than the kids. Sugar and rum." He winked.

A package was tied to one of Draken's blue-black horns. Reaching up, Maggie pulled it down, unwrapped the paper and opened the small box. Inside, nestled on the velvet, lay a stunning necklace. A deep blue surrounded by diamonds on a heavy silver chain. A question on her lips, he saved her from asking.

"The pendant is fabled to have belonged to a fae princess and said to give the wearer the ability to see the truth in all things. I thought you might like it."

Draken chuffed when Maggie kissed him on the nose and enthused, "It's so beautiful. I shall treasure it always, thank you."

Robert fastened the clasp and Maggie opened a stack of presents. Everything she could ever need for canning. She'd mentioned in passing she wanted to learn how to preserve the excess fruits and vegetables, so everyone pitched in for the supplies. And a note informed her someone would be coming to the house to teach her.

"What kind of jam shall I make first?"

Voices called out, and she smiled, thanking each person, wiping tears from her eyes.

Next, Fury ambled into the room. The hound was mythical. Midnight-black with three heads. Reputedly came from one of the deep circles of the Nether realm; loved to tear humans, Walkers, and other creatures to pieces, playing with them before devouring them, preferably with some type of tasty sauce. It was said in hushed whispers that the beast had the power to keep you alive so you knew you were being consumed. Worse, the monster actually talked!

Fury had lost a bet with Dayne, the nasty god of the Light realm and owed him one hundred years of service. With less than a year to go, Fury covertly switched sides after saving Maggie. What Dayne failed to realize was the phrasing was crucial when it came to terms. The demons were masters of properly wording curses and bargains...well, except for Solien. That demon spawn was a soldier without an original thought in his head. Fury had learned from the best and while he'd lost the bargain, he'd ensured the details weren't as bothersome as Dayne thought they were. While he couldn't eat the god or outright defy a properly worded order until the term was up, he had a certain latitude in how to interpret the orders he was given unless they were worded explicitly. And now he resided at Gwrych and watched over Maggie.

Between Fury, Draken and the other guests, there wasn't much space left. "My present to you is in Paris."

"Paris? When do we leave?"

He laughed. "Later. Not tonight. In the meantime, I thought it would suffice to tell you what the present is."

Robert was leaning in to hear, looking intrigued. Maggie clapped her hands together, practically vibrating off the floor.

"The suspense is killing me. What is it?"

The head with red eyes answered. "We ate the nasty Day Walker minions who tried to harm you last month and as a fitting tribute to our fondness for you, we put the bones in the Paris catacombs. We were out of wasabi sauce, we tried teriyaki. Not good. Not good at all."

Maggie giggled a sort of nervous laugh at Fury's idea of a "gift." The hound had an odd sense of humor. "No, I would think malt vinegar might have worked better on them."

The head with brown eyes looked thoughtful.

"I've never been to Paris. There are catacombs there?"

All three heads turned to look at her. The middle head was slightly larger, with gold eyes. "Never?"

Maggie shook her fire-engine red hair in the negative.

"Well, we'll remedy that. You'll enjoy Paris. And of course, we think you'll like seeing your name spelled out with your enemies' bones." At her startled look, the beast bobbed his middle head. "Don't worry, we did it in one of the tunnels off limits to tourists, though with over six million remains in the catacombs, it's unlikely anyone will stumble across our gift."

Well, it was the most unusual gift she'd ever received. And given her current company that was saying something. Deciding to go with it, she threw her arms around Fury, hugging each head. "I'm so glad you're on my side." Robert stifled a chuckle as she hugged him next and laughed. "The most amazing birthday ever."

Between them lay the inert green, their water... somewhere. "I hoped to..."

"Who... love?..."

He looked... since Mistress... in the... room, "I have it..."

Robert was bigger... in to... in looking forward. Maggie chin. I had made together, pro... reality, forgetting all medicine.

There... as if still... in the...

In Brad... with sad eyes however... "We are the party by... Walter nothing else tried to believe... in his fourth and as being... that all our looks as if you... we put the... in that I... tournament. We were out of wa..."

Ra... and Nor... could a...

Maggie spoke in tones... Laugh at... his words of a...

All three... house to...

❧ 8 ❧

Frederick skulked along the corridor. Mistress Abigail would be rolling over in her grave. Lord Colin had let a bunch of horrible children move into the castle. How could they take in orphans? Ravensmore was meant for nobility, not common peasant street urchins.

And he'd heard Robert took in a dragon at Gwrych. Let the creature move into one of the unused wings. What a filthy, foul beast. Thank god the beast wasn't at Ravensmore for it had the power to send him on to his final rest, and he wasn't ready to go. Frederick had too much to do. If the dragon showed up for Christmas Eve dinner it could ruin everything. He'd decided it would be his gift to Abigail to get rid of Emily. Somewhere in heaven he was sure she was looking down, in full approval of his actions.

With it being Christmas, no one would have their guard up or be paying attention to him. Colin might be angry about his latest pranks, especially after the incident with the twins. He smirked. That was a good one. The Baron would be occupied with the holiday and would leave Frederick alone. He always forgot about Frederick. Ignored him all these years. Never said a civil word. Killing Emily would ensure the Highlander got what he deserved.

When Emily took the nasty little twins out for a sleigh ride, it was the perfect opportunity. Yet the further she got from Ravensmore the less power he had. Enough to torment her but not enough to kill her. Frederick knew he could go as far as Castle Gloom, but his energy was weak, only allowing him to get there and back. The deed would have to be done here. At Ravensmore. Where he was strongest.

After the dinner celebration when everyone left, he'd do it then. Hmmm, he'd need to come up with a distraction to ensure Colin wasn't about. Wouldn't do to be thwarted so close to his goal. The ghost could taste victory. Rubbing his hands together in glee, Frederick vanished to the unused dungeon to plot.

CRYSTAL SHADOWS

❦ 9 ❦

"Wake up darlin'. Today is Christmas Eve, and we've lots to do before going to Ravensmore."

A grunt answered him. Chuckling, he threw the sheets off and jumped on the bed.

"Seriously? You are such a morning person. It's horrible."

His lady half-cracked an eye and scowled at him, grumbling under her breath.

"Fine. I'm getting up."

He passed a plate containing cut-up citrus under her nose, smiling as she sniffed deep. The other eye opened. "Is that grapefruit? All right. I'm up."

Stretching and yawning, Maggie staggered to the sitting area in front of the fire. One of his favorite shirts covered her. "Not so fast, my love." Picking her up, he settled her on his lap, reached out on the plate picking up half a grapefruit, and squeezed the juicy fruit. The juice ran down her bare creamy thigh, and he lifted her to lick it off. Popping the buttons, he tossed the shirt behind him. Taking another half of the juicy fruit, he drizzled the tartness down her breast. Reaching over, he sprinkled sugar on her nipple and bent his head, sucking. They sank to the floor, Maggie stroking him, guiding him to her, welcoming him home.

Finishing up breakfast, they showered together and descended the stairs to the sounds of kids running rampant. In the great hall, a huge fresh tree stood waiting to be dressed. Boxes of ornaments unearthed from one of the many storage rooms sat spilling decorations everywhere. Shouts of "it's about time" and "we ate ages ago" greeted them. Maggie moved among the children brushing a hand through the hair of one, patting the shoulder of another. Life was good.

Time for some order. Clapping his hands, Robert raised his voice.

"Right. You lot over there, take the lights and you lot there are in charge of the decorating."

A small voice called out, "Mr. Robert? We're not tall enough to reach all the way up, and the ladder isn't either."

A chuffing noise had every eye turning. "Never fear little ones. I'll fly you around."

Excited shouts filled the room. Leave it to Draken to make every child happy. "Line up. Everybody gets a turn." The children swarmed the dragon wanting to be first in line.

Hot chocolate and cookies were brought in for everyone. The kids shrieked and descended upon the treats like a swarm of locusts.

"This early in the morning? You'll spoil them," Maggie chided.

Robert's cook simply smiled and ate one of the cookies. "'Tis almost Christmas. Let the little monsters have sweets and treats all day today and tomorrow. They'll run off the excess energy at Ravensmore playing with the children there."

Robert chuckled and pinched Maggie on the bottom. "I'm not sure the kids even tasted the cookies."

The cook laughed and went back to the kitchen to start on lunch.

The day passed in a blur. Draken taught them Christmas carols. A dragon teaching children songs. What was next, Fury making sugar cookies? By the gods, how his life had changed. While he liked to grumble about the noise and mess the kids made, secretly he'd come to enjoy the entire package. Loved Gwrych filled to the rafters with love and laughter. There was plenty of room to take in more. Shaking his head, he joined in, adding a rich baritone to the music.

Lunch was served in one of the hothouses. The kids played hide and seek amongst the foliage. By late afternoon the tree was decorated. Calling for the lights to be dimmed, he spoke to everyone. "I couldn't be happier to have all of you here, together. This is your home, and I'm immensely happy to have all of you living at Gwrych. Now, sweet Jamie, will you do the honors and light her up?"

The boy ran and plugged the tree in. White lights sparkled and filled the room along with the "oohs" and "ahhs" of the children.

"Seems we're missing one thing." The lights hit Draken's scales, reflecting a rainbow of blues across the stone walls and floor. "Miss Melody, would you like to put the star on the top?"

The little girl shrieked with delight and ran to the dragon. Robert put her on Draken's back, handing her the stuffed cat she always dragged around. The crystal star he placed in her lap.

The stuffed animal was dingy and tattered, but the kid loved it. Hell, in her animal wish list not only had she asked for cats and dogs but for pigs and chickens. He sighed, backing away, picturing a pig following her around the house.

Draken leapt into the air, wings unfurling and glided to the top of the tree to place the star on the very top.

Everyone bundled up and filed outside to climb into the waiting bus and SUV. They'd caravan to Ravensmore. Colin told him about the nasty ghost who used to wait on Abigail and was now terrorizing the household in his ghostly form. If Colin hadn't already banished the spirit, Robert would help him finish the deed after dinner.

❧ 10 ❦

Hamish dematerialized from his townhouse in Edinburgh to the shopping area surrounding the Leith Docks. He was restless thinking about Emily's offer to come to Ravensmore for Christmas Eve dinner. The nerve of the chit. Whenever he needed to work something out, he walked.

While he didn't feel the cold or any temperature for that matter, it wouldn't do for tourists to see him walking down the street shirtless and, for some reason he didn't understand he wanted to be seen. Dressed in dark tailored jeans, Doc Martens, a charcoal sweater, and leather trench coat he caught sight of himself reflected in a tavern window and frowned. To any outsider he looked respectable, yet all he could see were haunted green eyes looking back at him. A small boy around the age of seven ran in front of him chasing his hat. Hamish's step faltered. He felt as if someone had driven a dagger into his gut. The pain quick and intense. Staggering over to a bench overlooking the water he sunk down oblivious to the happy shoppers going about their business.

Memories came rolling in like a landslide buffeting him to and fro. Helpless to stop them, he let the images take him.

'Twas shortly after his seventh birthday. Hamish had

unearthed an ancient dagger fragment digging around the western wall of Ravensmore Castle. Anxious to show his father he ran to the study. Reaching out to knock, he heard his brother's voice. Colin was excited. Hamish pressed his ear to the keyhole.

Baron Campbell's voice was thick with emotion. "Colin, your mother and I were verra blessed the day she birthed you. You're growing into a young man we are proud of. Our favorite son. We have great expectations for you, lad. Always take care of your birthright and its inhabitants, and Ravensmore will stand for a thousand years." Their father continued, sighing as if the weight of the world was bearing down on him. "Watch over Hamish. The lad is lazy. All he wants to do is play, ride horses and steal sweets from Cook. Not to mention he's a bit dim-witted. He'll never amount to anything, so you must do your duty and look out for him always."

"He can't help what he is. I promise to look after him," Colin answered in a solemn voice.

Hamish reeled back from the door. Colin was the favorite. They thought Hamish was lazy and stupid. He tried to please his parents, but they always brushed him off. Just the previous week his family visited those in the village, bestowing a few coins here and there, inquiring after their tenants.

When his family left they never bothered to tell him. Hamish was left behind. Didn't they wonder why he wasn't in the carriage? He had to walk all afternoon and night before he staggered in the next morning. Cold, dirty, and hungry, he went to the kitchens to eat when the cook shrieked at him and called for his mother. Instead of being worried, she was angry he'd ripped his shirt. Angry he was dirty. She sent him to bed for the day without any food.

He'd always suspected they liked his elder brother more, but to say it out loud somehow seemed wrong. Shouldn't parents love both their children equally?

Dropping the ancient fragment, it clattered to the stone floor as Hamish fled outside to the stables and his horse.

The horn from a ship coming into port sounded pulling Hamish out of the painful memory. All he'd wanted was his parents to love him. What was wrong with him that even as a small child they despised him so? Hamish was the "spare heir." A backup in case the unthinkable happened.

Mouth pulling up into a sneer, he caught sight of a pick-pocket, well, mugger was the current term, and narrowed his eyes. The small-time predator would make a good appetizer before dinner. Dematerializing, he followed the man, invisible to all.

❧ 11 ❧

L eaving Gwrych, the kids were excited to visit another
castle and to play with other children. They laughed
and sang on the way to Ravensmore.

The roads were clear. During the days since the winter
solstice it had grown colder, and snow blanketed the land. The
late afternoon sky promised more to come. Fury and Draken
poofed there while Maggie and Robert rode in a car with some
of the munchkins while the rest were in a bus they'd bought for
the occasion. There were lots of "oohs" and "ahhs" when they
pulled up the drive. Ravensmore was a forbidding structure built
of gray stone and sat on the edge of a cliff, looking down on all
who approached. Behind the castle lay the sea and in front, open
ground swept down to the forest.

"Wow. Colin's castle is beautiful and a little bit scary." Maggie
turned her face to Robert, placing a hand on his knee. "Don't
worry, I like Gwrych better."

The muscles in his knee relaxed. Glad she favored his home
more than Colin's.

Colin's butler opened the door, greeting the raucous bunch.
"So pleased you all could make it. If you'll follow me. Everyone's
in the great hall."

46

Using his power to turn the noise inside his head down, Robert followed behind, smiling at the children.

Music wafted down the corridor. A small orchestra was set up in a corner of the great hall playing Christmas tunes. The large room was decorated with an enormous tree and greenery on the walls and mantle. The huge hearth was lit and the fire cast dancing shadows on the walls. Colin's housekeeper fussed over the little ones, bringing spiced cider and the ingredients for them to make s'mores. Laughing when one shrieked as their marshmallow caught fire or fell into the flames.

Robert spotted his human friend. "Monroe. Good to see you, mate. I see you've found the good stuff." Robert clapped him on the back. The ex-cop's turquoise eyes were slightly bloodshot, his dirty blond hair looked in need of a good washing. Frowning, Robert held his tongue.

Holding up a glass of Ravensmore whisky, Monroe smiled. "Aye. Merry Christmas to you both." After hugging Maggie and kissing her on the cheek, he leaned in close to whisper to Robert in a slightly slurred voice. "Did you know Fury looks human? With only one head?"

The corner of his mouth turned up. "He'd look rather ridiculous with three heads, wouldn't he?" Absently patting Maggie on the rear as she left to greet Emily, Robert studied the now private investigator. The guy was usually solid but over the last few months he'd lost weight, looked a bit haggard. "He decided it was best to show up in human form and not scare those who hadn't met him before. Though I wonder what happens to the other two heads when he looks like the rest of us?"

"It's...well, I guess I was a bit surprised to see him looking human." Monroe scratched his unshaven chin while looking over at Fury, who was at this moment building a large Lego tower and bridge with some of the kids.

Robert could hear him telling a story of sacking ancient Greece and eating the residents. The beast had a thing for putting various sauces on his food before he ate.

"Where's Draken?"

Robert laughed. "Outside eating. He'll be in afterwards. It would be a mite unpleasant for the little ones to see him enjoying a meal up close and personal."

"Dragons and hellhounds. It's been an interesting year." Monroe slapped him on the shoulder.

Robert wandered over to speak to Colin and Jasper when Monroe was summoned by a few of the kids to help with the Lego towers.

"Robert. Glad you could make it." Colin pulled him into a hug.

Jasper kissed him on each cheek. Jasper was a Shadow Walker based in Paris. In a former life he'd been a soldier. Now he was a soldier of a different kind.

"Mon ami, so nice to see you and Maggie." Jasper handed him a glass of dark red wine. "From my estate. Enjoy."

It was like liquid velvet and tasted faintly of honey and cherries. "'Tis excellent. I'll have to buy a few cases from you."

"No need. They've been loaded into your vehicle. Merry Christmas."

Robert inclined his head. "All this time, so many years passing, and none of us ever got together to celebrate. Must be Emily and Maggie's influence."

Colin cleared his throat. "Thank the gods for them both. Holidays are a time for family. I want you both to know...I consider you my family. Brothers."

There was a lot of looking around the room and the discreet eye wipe going on. Before things could get emotional Colin left to break up a minor scuffle between two of the older boys, and Jasper shot Robert a pointed look.

"He doesn't know Hamish is back? Why haven't you told him? It's been months since I ran into him in Paris. Thought he was Colin at first."

"I was going to. But decided I'd wait until after the holiday. Why on earth would Thorne make him one of us? I've been trying to get an answer, but the blasted god always changes the subject. He knows Hamish killed Colin, how much they hate each other."

"I won't say a word, but Colin is going to go ballistic when he finds out." They watched Colin across the room and spent the next hour talking about recent events and the worsening state of the world. Speculating as to why Thorne had been so distant and distracted lately. Wondering what Dayne and his merry band of misfits would do next.

Jasper wandered off to peruse Colin's extensive wine cellar leaving Robert to his thoughts. He didn't want to tell everyone about Frederick so when Colin left the kids to refill his drink Robert met him by the sideboard, perusing the selections.

Looking around to make sure they weren't overheard, Robert told Colin the tale.

"Colin, Maggie had a run-in with that nasty Frenchman of yours. Scared the hell out of her. Walking down the hallway, she stopped when she saw ice coating the wall, table and mirror. Moving closer, she looked in the mirror, the surface showed her a version of herself as if she'd aged a hundredfold. I heard her scream, and when I looked there was no ice." Robert paused, drinking his whisky.

"The wall was wet, water dripped down but nothing else was amiss other than a sizeable puddle on the floor. To make things worse, on the way in, I'd stopped for a moment listening to one of the kids and the bastard tripped her in the hallway as she went to say hello to Emily. She's fine but gave her a terrible fright. From what you've told me, he's getting worse. Seems to be intent on causing harm to all who live at or visit Ravensmore."

Clenching his jaw, Colin looked around to see where his wife was. Seeing her deep in conversation with Maggie, he turned back to Robert. "The French bastard has been busy. Yesterday I heard one of the children screaming. Frederick made the child's sugar cookies look rotten. Not only that, when Emily picked up the plate to take it to the dining room, the spirit made it look like worms covered the plate of cookies. The plate was covered in ice when she dropped it on the floor. Thank goodness it was metal, or Emily might have been cut by the shards. When she looked again, the cookies were untouched though in pieces all over the kitchen floor. You should have heard the creative swear words."

Colin grimaced. "Emily called the dogs in to clean up the pieces on the floor. If that little incident wasn't bad enough he's been scaring the children and the French bastard ripped up all of Emily's clothes." Colin ran his hands through his hair trying to rein in his temper.

"But worst of all...he made the twins look dead when she went for a walk. Scared her to death. It made her verra angry. She threatened to make me sleep on the couch if I don't get rid of the ghost. 'Tis rather strange, but ice appears on everything when it happens. Since I canna kill him with my bare hands, I was going to banish him, and the wanker used a mirror to deflect the net I cast. You're right. 'Tis past time for him to go on to the next realm."

"I wonder why the ice? That's new, isn't it?" Robert rubbed his chin thinking as Colin nodded.

"With your help we'll take care of him after dinner. It's high time Frederick was gone." If Colin had his way the hateful spirit would have been banished the day Thorne brought him back to life but he never seemed to find the time to get rid of Frederick.

Looking across the room, Robert looked for Maggie. "Where's my wife? Did you see her leave?"

Colin's response was a negative. Was there more trouble with that strutting ninny, Frederick?

12

Frederick planned the perfect distraction. It was so good he'd have the chance to kill not only Emily but Maggie as well. Not that he had anything against the woman other than she was married to Robert and therefore it would hurt the pirate deeply. Good. He deserved to be as tormented as Frederick was. Robert was responsible for Abigail's death. Not directly, but it was he who took her. She'd been on a ship bound for the West Indies to marry a wealthy plantation owner after she'd had Hamish murdered. Robert intercepted the ship and sold Frederick's fine lady to a doddering old Lord looking for a maid. Yes, it was a fine house, but the slight was unforgivable. Abigail died a year later from a tropical fever.

Robert needed to pay. And Emily. She was a horrible American who wasn't fit to reside over Ravensmore. How dare she bring nasty little children into the castle.

Grumbling as he drifted along, Frederick came to one of the unused rooms. The door was ajar. A mountain of presents waited inside. There were a few large items waiting to be put together but the rest were prettily wrapped.

Not for long.

Feelings of glee ran through him or what he thought glee

must feel like. He'd ruin Christmas and murder both ladies. Why it was like the time he'd found out his mentor had murdered that little housemaid.

Mr. White was the spirit's name. Frederick could see him on account of him almost dying and coming back from the flu as a small child in France. At the castle, Mr. White had been the original lady's servant to the first mistress of Ravensmore. No one at the castle seemed to be able to see him except Frederick. Mr. White hated Hamish and when he found out the young man had gotten the girl in a family way, he took care of the matter. The best part—Mr. White made himself look like Hamish so the girl thought Hamish was the one who murdered her. It was fantastic revenge on the wastrel son.

Assured no one was in the hallway outside, Frederick set to work. He manifested into physical form and tore the beautiful paper and ribbon to shreds, throwing it around the room with abandon. Stomping on the boxes, destroying everything he could. Anything breakable, he threw to the stone floor. The plastic toys he hit with a bit of energy only enough to melt them into worthless junk. Not wanting to risk expending too much power, Frederick left the smoking mess and dematerialized to the battlements. He needed to conserve his strength otherwise he wouldn't have enough to carry out the rest of his delightful plans.

THORNE REQUIRED TIME TO THINK BEFORE HE JOINED HIS men. Throughout his existence, no one had ever invited Thorne to celebrate Christmas. The women Colin and Robert married were having an interesting effect on his warriors—bringing out their humanity. Materializing to the battlements at Ravensmore to clear his head, he sank down on a stone bench, hidden from prying eyes.

His peace was short-lived.

What was this? From the shadows Thorne watched the ghost appear. The spirit seemed rather pleased with himself.

"What are you doing up here?" Frederick said, peering into the shadows. "I don't recognize you. Ravensmore belongs to me so if you know what's good for you, you better leave now before things take an ugly turn."

Thorne arched a brow. An arrogant spirit with diminished power and one who didn't recognize the god of shadow. Wondering what game was afoot, Thorne looked inside the ghost seeing what tricks he'd been up to.

"You are nothing more than an ant under my shoe. All spirits are under the control of the god of shadow. Maybe it's high time you learned a lesson or better yet, time to move on to the final realm."

Now the wretched spirit looked worried. "I've never seen you before but all have heard tale of your powers. Please forgive my mistake." The ghost sketched a small bow. "My name is Frederick. I watch over the ladies of Ravensmore."

"Really?" Thorne couldn't keep the sarcasm from his voice. "I'd say you like to cause chaos and destruction. Hardly qualifies as 'watching over.' Not to mention I know what you did to the children's presents." Thorne cut his eyes to the ghost. "On Christmas Eve, no less. Trying to be a new kind of Scrooge, are you?"

Frederick had the grace to look the tiniest bit abashed. Otherwise, Thorne would have fried him, sending him on to his final rest without a second thought. But it was Christmas. So instead he'd try to get into the spirit so to speak. "Cause any further problems and I'll send you on to the final realm."

The ghost bowed low to the ground. "Of course, your grace."

"Get out of here before I change my mind." Thorne growled as the spirit vanished.

He decided to go and see if the pictures in the spirits' consciousness were as bad as they looked.

Appearing in the corridor outside the room, Thorne paused.

Satisfied no one was about, he slipped inside shutting the door from prying eyes and cursed under his breath. The spirit hadn't been exaggerating. The toys were destroyed. Melted. All the boxes, ribbons, and paper in bits and pieces, scattered across the room. Even the dolls had their heads ripped off. This wouldn't do at all.

Summoning power, Thorne looked into the past, watched the presents brought in and stacked high. Watched as Emily and Colin wrapped each one. They'd clearly put a great deal of thought into finding the right gift for each child. Power swelled, sending lightning flashing across the stone walls. Thunder rumbled, and Thorne sent out a command to smother the sounds from anyone outside the room. The wind began to blow, pieces of torn paper and ribbon swirling around faster and faster.

Broken and melted toys joined in and soon the room looked like a tornado of holiday trash. Pushing outward on his power, it grew warm in the room, the lightning making the dark room look like the brightest day at the beach. The smell of plastic filled the air as toys changed, the damage undone as they returned to their natural state. Toys returned to unblemished boxes, heads reappeared on dolls, crushed pieces of glass and pottery reformed. Exhaling, his power surged, and the wrapping paper and ribbon recovered the boxes each one stacking neatly into a pile.

Finished he sent his power back to the source and took a look around. The room was as it had been before Frederick made a mess of it. Colin and Emily would never know. No need to spoil anyone's holiday.

With a half-smile he added a few of his own gifts for the children. Realizing it was growing late, Thorne willed himself to the library to greet his hosts.

✷ 13 ✷

The mugger had been merely an appetizer. Hamish hated the holidays, and Christmas was the worst of the lot. Thieves, rapists, and other predators were out looking for an easy score while shoppers frantically finished last-minute purchases before rushing home to spend Christmas Eve with loved ones.

Loved ones. What exactly did that mean? It sure as hell didn't define his parents. Hamish's tenth birthday was a perfect example of their "love."

His parents had been in London for a month visiting friends. He recalled the day they left. Hamish knocked on his mother's bedroom door. She was with her maids picking out which jewelry to take with her. She looked up. "What do you want?"

"Mother, will you and Father be back in time for my birthday?"

She sounded exasperated when she turned to look at him. "Honestly. Isn't it enough I almost died giving birth to you? We provide for you, clothe and feed you, and it's never enough. You always want more." She slammed the pearls down on the table. "These are important connections your father is making in London. To benefit us all. How can you be so ungrateful?" The baroness rubbed her temples. "Now look what you've done. Given me a terrible headache. I'll have to suffer it all day today." She shooed him away, not even hugging him goodbye.

His parents never hugged him.

Every day he'd waited for his parents to return. They were supposed to be back on his name day. Today was the day. Colin gave him an old sword he'd found buried at Castle Gloom. Knew how much Hamish loved old relics. He and Colin swore they'd be brothers forever but lately...Colin seemed to always be in the right while Hamish was the one continually punished. His brother was older by five years and a man at fifteen.

The sound of a door sent him running down the stairs to the great hall. It wasn't his parents just a friend of Colin's.

"Stay out of trouble, little brother." Colin hurried past Hamish as he stood alone in the hall.

"Colin, wait." His brother turned. Impatience clear on his face. "I thought—with our parents gone that you'd spend the day with me...for my birthday." Hamish hated the needy, wistful tone of his voice.

Colin and his friend laughed. "Don't be a baby. Go play with the sword I gave you. I've other things to do." And with that his brother strode out of the hall, shutting the door with a bang.

Shoulders sagging, Hamish ran to the unused nursery. When he couldn't bear his family for one more instant, he'd escape to this haven. Over the last two years he'd made it his own, dragging unwanted furniture into the room to display all of his unearthed treasures.

The time passed quickly, and two weeks after his birthday, his parents returned. No mention was made of his name day. A few days later, Hamish found his father in his study after dinner. He knocked at the door.

"Aye. Come in."

All day long Hamish had worked up the courage to face his father. A slight tremor to his right hand was the only sign Hamish was nervous.

"Father. I was wondering if we might celebrate my birthday? I turned ten three weeks ago today."

The fearsome Baron Campbell looked at his son. "Aren't you getting a bit old to be expecting birthday celebrations?"

"We had a verra large party for Colin's birthday last year."

His father turned the full force of his gaze upon his son. Gulping, Hamish stood firm, knees knocking together. "Colin is my firstborn. Heir to Ravensmore. Everything I do is to prepare him to take my place as the next Baron Campbell." His father sighed and ran his hands through his hair. "'Tis past time for you to grow up and stop playing with childish things. Don't think I don't know about your playroom in the old nursery."

At Hamish's panicked look, his father continued. "I've had everything in the room destroyed. You are not to go there again. And there will be no more talk of birthdays or of your elder brother. Why can't you be more like Colin?" Not waiting for an answer, he turned his attention back to the papers on his desk. "Now leave me be."

The sounds of modern-day life drew him out of the memories and into the present. Lip curling in disgust, he dematerialized to Ravensmore.

It was time for Christmas dinner.

ICED IN SHADOW

❧ 14 ❧

Inside Ravensmore dinner was announced. Frederick made himself transparent and hovered above the entryway. He wanted to ice everyone who walked through the doors to the great hall but then he'd give himself away. There was one thing he could do...smirking, he drifted down under the tables icing the floor.

EMILY AND MAGGIE RETURNED WHISPERING ABOUT THE GIFTS they'd found for their respective husbands. Seeing Robert's worried look, Emily spoke up. "Maggie and I had some secret holiday stuff to take care of. No need to worry your pretty little head."

Robert gave Colin a look that said, *how do you put up with her?* and walked towards them, kissing Maggie, dipping her back as the children made kissing noises and yelled "eww," "gross," and other jests.

"Glad you're all right. When I didn't see you earlier I wondered where you'd gone to. Don't want anything happening to my lady."

Colin joined in the conversation. "Frederick is on the rampage so until we have him in hand I'd prefer no one wanders about alone."

"Of course, dear." Emily gave him a big kiss and hug and led the way to dinner.

The children ran shrieking and laughing to the tables in the great hall.

Long wooden tables and comfortable chairs had been set up spanning the hall. The tables were set with festive greenery and ribbon. The china was white with blue and green flowers and vines around the border. In the middle of each cluster of the flower centerpiece was the Ravensmore crest. The crystal sparkled in the glow of the candles and sconces on the walls. A magnificent chandelier twinkled above them. The sterling flatware turned to burnished silver in the flickering light. The cloth napkins alternated between blue and green.

Some of the children seemed nervous and Emily walked among them reassuring them. Telling them not to worry about the stuffy old dishes.

It took a moment for Emily to realize what was happening. People were slipping and falling as they sat down. The kids shrieking and then laughing.

"Damn it!" She met Colin's eyes and pointed towards the study a tiny bit gratified when he paled. That's right, she thought. Banish this sonofabitch tonight or you'll be sleeping on the couch until it's done.

Lifting the heavy tablecloths there was a thin layer of ice under every chair. As she watched it melted, leaving the floor wet.

"Mrs. Emily, you said a bad word!' A couple of the children were looking at her, huge smiles across their tiny faces.

"I did. Sorry. Guess I'll have to put a pound in the swear jar."

Giggling, the kids scampered to tell their friends.

Thorne clapped his hands. The room fell silent except for

the Christmas music. "The mess is gone. Everyone take your seats." The god looked to Colin. "Trouble, Highlander?"

"No. I've got it under control."

Emily barely resisted snorting upon hearing her husband's answer. Nodding to the servers to begin, she vowed to be pleasant during dinner. Not to let Frederick ruin her dinner.

Wine from Jasper's estate was served to the adults while the kids enjoyed apple cider. The food kept coming and coming. Starting with fruit and cheese, progressing to soup and salad, then on to roasted venison, filet mignon, ham and turkey. Emily was astonished at the sheer volume of food in front of them. The cook had outdone herself this time. There were mashed potatoes, asparagus with hollandaise sauce, shrimp cocktail, rolls, freshly churned butter, dressing, and yams. Some of the kids eyes were huge, taking in the feast before them. Emily wondered if they'd ever seen so much food.

Her heart clenched thinking of the hard life some of the children had experienced. This would be a new start. Here they would be cherished. Throat tightening up, she took a quick sip of water and smiled at her other half.

They had electricity, but Colin loved candlelight so most of the lights were dimmed and candles flickered everywhere casting the party back in time.

The room was cozy with the fire crackling and the smell of the freshly cut tree and greenery filling the room. The orchestra played Christmas carols and her sexy husband pushed his chair back, standing.

She never tired of looking at him. All hard muscle and a strong face made of angles and planes. His scar stood out tonight. It ran from his forehead, through part of his eyebrow, down his cheekbone and ended at his ear. She'd spent many hours tracing it with her fingertip while they were in bed together.

Colin cleared his throat. "We thank ye for coming to celebrate Christmas Eve with us. For those who've come to live here at Ravensmore, we are verra happy you're here, safe and sound. To Robert and Maggie for opening Gwrych up and to those living there, we welcome you to the family. For helping Maggie's friends and those in need, my brother in arms, Jasper, I thank you. Monroe—you've proven yerself friend to us and have our friendship in return."

Monroe was sitting across from her or Emily would have missed the look of surprise on his face. Her husband and the investigator had never gotten along but since Monroe had been working with them, he softened and decided the guy was all right.

"To Fury and Draken, your friendship is most appreciated. You are always welcome here. And to Billy. Without whom Emily might have been lost." Seeing a few confused faces, he elaborated.

"Billy was born at Ravensmore a long time ago. He fell down the stairs one night and broke his neck. My ancestor was verra fond of him and had a small statue commissioned and placed in the kitchen garden as a memorial. He was buried in our family graveyard. 'Tis said he appears whenever there is danger to Ravensmore or those who live here. I know this to be true." Stopping, Colin looked at each face.

"Raise your glass—join me in a moment of silence for those we've lost. To Kendrick, not only one of the finest warriors I've had the pleasure to fight beside but a good man. He is deeply missed." Everyone raised their glass, even the children, sensing it was something important. Thorne nodded at his men. Silence filled the room, stretching before Colin broke it. "Merry Christmas."

The orchestra started back up. Dinner was perfect. Emily had a moment of sadness for the loss of her parents. She felt it more during the holidays. But now she had a big family and they needed her.

After dinner, the dishes were cleared away and in rolled a cart brimming with dessert, pushed by two of the kitchen workers. It was laden with apple pie, sugared cranberries, chocolate fudge, cookies and cheesecake. The kids were ecstatic. Champagne flowed and everyone ate at least two pieces of dessert.

Afterwards the kids went off to play and the adults retired to the library for whisky and cognac. Entering the library, Emily jumped seeing Thorne sprawled in one of the chairs staring into the flames. He must have left dinner early without her noticing. He looked the calmest she'd ever seen him. Maybe the holiday was good for everyone.

A time to reflect, to spend time with those we care about. A time of renewal.

Emily went and hugged him, surprised when he returned the hug. Normally he shrank away. Guess everybody had the holiday spirit. Settling in the comfy chairs beside the fire, she caught up with Maggie while Thorne bid them goodnight and left to talk with his men.

Hamish hadn't shown up. She'd hoped he'd come and start down the path of forgiveness and second chances. Make things right with Colin. Maybe he'd show up for Christmas day. She had presents for him. Colin would be angry but in time, he'd mend fences with his brother. She'd talked with him a great deal and thought she detected a small willingness to at least consider the idea.

The smallest ember could lead to the largest fire. Sometimes it just took someone else to fan the flames.

❧ 15 ❧

Outside Ravensmore, the wind picked up, snow swirling, coming down in big, fluffy flakes. Hamish stood on the terrace where he had a clear view of the occupants inside. What a cozy scene. All of them together, laughing and having a good time. And there was his brother. The one who always had everything when they were growing up. The favorite. Hamish was the spare heir, nothing more. Ignored. Forgotten. Fast forward hundreds of years and nothing had changed. Colin was still the golden boy. Holding court.

If Colin cared, he would have come to see Hamish at Gloom but not a word. Now Emily expected him to show up and join the party as if nothing had ever happened?

Hamish didn't believe Colin would forgive him. Not for killing him. There were too many hurts, and some wounds never healed. Every time he thought he could begin again with Colin, something happened, and Hamish went right back to familiar feelings...anger and hurt. Maybe someday he could change but not today.

Colin's pretty little wife was way off base on this one. As if hearing his thoughts, at that moment Thorne looked up and out the window at him. Like he could see Hamish standing outside

63

in the shadows. Narrowing his eyes, Thorne stared a moment longer. Then the spell was broken as Jasper said something and the god turned away.

No longer would he be forgotten. Pushed aside. Scowling, Hamish turned away from the golden light spilling out. He turned, stared into the darkness for several minutes, wrestling with his thoughts before giving up and dematerializing back to Gloom.

❧ 16 ❧

Thorne made his excuses early and vanished. The kids were busy playing. Fury and Draken left for Gwrych whispering about some "gift" they were finishing. Emily and Maggie were off plotting again. While Jasper and Monroe debated whose team had a better chance at the World Cup, Colin and Robert decided it was time and went in search of Frederick.

"After that stunt at dinner, Frederick will know we're after him. Best try Abigail's old rooms first." Colin led the way. The hallway was quiet. None of the rooms in the corridor providing shelter to the evil spirit.

A commotion downstairs sent Colin and Robert dematerializing to the first floor. The housekeeper ran towards them, face pale.

"M'lord, come quickly."

Fear snaked down Colin's spine. They followed her through the kitchen to the passage leading to the storage area. There were three chambers. One was used for refrigeration, one for freezing, and the last for ice. It was so cold in the stone under Ravensmore where the seawater flowed underneath the castle, it created ideal temperatures. Wine was stored there along with homemade cheese.

The woman was wringing her hands. "I came in to get some chocolate ice cream for the kids, and I saw this." She pointed to the corner of the chamber.

The stone floor and walls were coated in ice. Large ice blocks took up half of the room and crude shelves had been carved into the stone hundreds of years ago, creating ideal storage areas. But what drew Colin's attention was in the center of the floor.

A black scuffed leather boot and blue and gray scarf. "By the gods, that's Emily's scarf."

Robert swore in five languages. "Maggie's boot." He paced the cavernous room. "Frederick has them."

Colin turned to his housekeeper. "Please go check on the children. Make sure everyone is accounted for."

The odd thing was he didn't feel any change in his heartbeat. With he and Emily sharing one heart, he should feel a rapid heartbeat or some other indicator. She wasn't dead because if she was he would have already dropped where he stood. So either she was unafraid or unconscious.

"Damnation. Robert, we'll have Jasper and Monroe check the outbuildings while we go back upstairs. That lousy French bastard has to be close."

His middle-aged housekeeper brushed the stray hair escaping her bun before she turned around halfway up the steps. "Monroe already left. Jasper is watching over the kids."

"Tell him what's happened and that Robert and I have gone to search upstairs. Have him stay with the kids in case Frederick comes after them. He can protect you all."

She nodded and hurried up the stairs.

Colin looked to his brother-in-arms. "We'll meet by Abigail's old rooms." Nodding, they vanished.

Standing in the hallway outside his ex-fiancé's room, it was quiet. "I've been meaning to update this entire wing for more children." Colin managed a grin. "That scheming bitch hated kids. I think it's a fitting ending for her and Frederick. Shall we go in?"

"Hell, yes." Robert shed his human form as Colin followed suit. Changing into energy, they slid through the heavy wood door. Being unable to communicate in this form wouldn't matter. Both knew what needed to be done. Find the women and destroy the enemy. The bedroom was still, waiting. Colin's consciousness sensed an energy signature coming from the bathroom and another from the wardrobe.

Moving to the wardrobe Colin could sense his beloved. Reforming, he eased the door open. Robert took human form beside him. Inside the two women were bound and gagged. Maggie had a bump above her eyebrow but otherwise seemed unharmed. Emily sported a bruise on her chin.

Colin cut the bindings and motioned for them to be quiet. He picked up Emily while Robert carried Maggie outside to the hallway. Colin left the door slightly ajar as sounds of Frederick singing loudly drifted out, echoing in the bathroom.

"What the bloody hell happened?" Colin held Emily close. "Thank the gods."

"I'll kill the wanker..." Robert trailed off, stroking Maggie's cheek.

Maggie spoke first. "We'd gone to the ice room to talk about your Christmas presents when out of nowhere *he* appeared. Before I knew what had happened, I felt my head explode, and the next thing I knew I was in this damn wardrobe. Why does that deranged Frenchman still dress like it's four hundred years ago?" She rolled her eyes. "The door opened, and he tossed Emily in like a sack of potatoes. She hit the wall face first."

Emily added to the conversation. "That nutcase told us he was going to throw us off the battlements and watch us die. I wanted to tell him good luck with that since we're immortal but thought he might cut our heads off or something. He was muttering 'Let them eat cake', or some such nonsense so I decided it best not to make the crazy person any crazier."

Maggie finished the story. "Then you found us."

"Are the babies unharmed?"

"They're sound asleep and fine." Colin reassured Emily.

"What about the rest of the children?" Maggie and Emily asked at the same time.

Robert kissed Maggie, pulling her tight against him. "Never fear, ladies. Jasper has them in hand."

"You'd better take care of this problem once and for all. I'd hate for you to spend the rest of the year on the couch." Emily glared at Colin.

"The couch! Robert's going to sleep with the animals if this isn't finished tonight." Maggie smacked him on the shoulder.

Colin held his hands up in surrender. "If you're both well enough, please go downstairs with Jasper and the children so Robert and I can end this."

Emily and Maggie left with annoyed looks on their faces. Colin spoke first. "I don't know why they didn't allow women to fight back in the day. Those two could have routed any enemy without breaking a sweat."

"They are rather terrifying when they're angry." Robert rubbed his shoulder. "Let's get this done."

Reforming into energy, they drifted to the bathroom. The singing had given way to mumblings. The ghost was sprawled out in the tub, drinking a bottle of expensive wine from the cellar and talking to himself.

"All I've done for Mistress Abigail, and no one appreciates it. I've kept those other women, those imposters out of her chambers and what do I get? The Mighty Colin wants to destroy me. He doesn't understand what I need to do. That I must keep protecting the memory of you, Mistress Abigail. But never fear my dear lady, after I've had a few more drinks I shall throw Colin's and Robert's wives off the battlements into the sea. I think it's a fitting ending on Christmas Eve. Will ruin the holiday for all. I know you would approve." Frederick toasted the air and continued to drink.

Positioning himself at the front of the claw foot tub, Colin and Robert took shape and before Frederick could lower the glass, sent out a blast of energy. It shimmered in the dim light, hues of blue and silver mixed with Robert's purple and gold, forming into a sparkling net, settling over the startled spirit.

Frederick shrieked and thrashed. "Let me go you whoresons. I've not finished my duties. I must stay and protect her memory. I promised Abigail. I promised Mr. White I'd never give up."

"Who is Mr. White?" Colin was puzzled. 'Twas the first time he'd ever heard the name.

"Let me out of this trap, and I'll tell you everything. Even where your lovely wives are." Frederick's sly response made Colin's blood boil.

"We've seen to our ladies." Robert shot a stinging bolt of energy into the ghost.

Frederick shrieked in pain. "Let me go. I've work to do."

"Enough," Colin bellowed. "Tell me about Mr. White or be sent to your final rest now."

Frederick pouted and stopped struggling. "You made me spill my wine." Fumbling around he inspected the empty glass, shrugged and tossed it away. It shattered on the stone floor next to the tub. Next, he pulled the half-empty bottle from the bottom of the net and took a swig. "Mr. White was the first lady's servant to the first mistress of Ravensmore. He committed many wonderful acts. When he went on to the great final rest, I promised I'd see to it that Ravensmore had a proper French mistress and that all others would be taken care of. I've failed him." Frederick sniffled.

"Oh, for the seven hells, shut up," Robert muttered as the ghost begged and pleaded to be let go.

"You've caused too many problems. Hurt Emily. Hurt Maggie. Scared those under my protection. I should have banished you a long time ago," Colin growled.

Frederick tried to ice the net, but the ice melted as quickly as it touched the pulsing structure, hissing as the hot droplets fell into the tub. Seeing he had no way out, Frederick favored Colin with a look so full of malice Colin almost reached out and punched the bastard.

"Any last words?" Robert used his energy to tighten the net.

As Colin began the incantation, the evil spirit took one last look at them and spat the words, "Too bad you don't know the real story of the servant girl's death. Or your mother's."

The incantation of old Latin words complete, Colin couldn't stop it to find out what he meant. His mother's death? The servant girl's? What would Frederick know about that? Was he involved? It was too late to find out. The banishment was complete.

With a pop and a hiss, the ghost vanished, shrieking, "Nooo!" The energy net dissipated.

Robert clapped him on the back. "Well done. I need a drink. Shall we?"

Colin nodded, deep in thought.

❧ 17 ❧

I n the blink of an eye, the clock struck ten and everyone said their goodbyes as Colin and Robert reappeared.

Emily raised her eyebrows.

Colin nodded.

Good it was done. She felt a weight lift.

The kids protested until being reminded they needed to get to bed so Santa could come.

Colin thanked Jasper, who hugged him before disappearing back to Paris.

Robert and Colin had loads of gifts to bring out and place under the trees. Bundling everyone into the vehicles, they headed out into the night. Snowflakes the size of Olympic medals were falling, giving the scene a fairytale look.

Satisfied everyone was safely off, Emily turned to Colin. "Let's get these little ones to bed so we can finish putting out the presents. Then I have a special present for you, husband..." She laughed and dematerialized them to the storage room where the gifts were hidden.

"Does this mean I don't have to sleep on the couch tonight?"

"Depends on how well you ravish me." She waggled her eyebrows at the man who stole her breath away. Emily's laugh died a moment later when Colin used his power to remove their clothing, manifesting a soft rug underneath them. Looking up, seeing the love in his eyes reflected back, she wanted to scream her happiness for all the world to know.

With a wicked grin, Colin covered her body reaching between them, seeking her heat. When he stroked her center Emily moaned and stretched her heels wide, giving him complete access. He slid down her body, a deep rumble emanating from him.

A cool breeze blew across her skin doing nothing to cool the fire burning throughout her body. Emily ran her hands through Colin's hair, marveling at the silken strands, clenching handfuls as the vibration from his growl against her bud sent her spinning into bliss, arching underneath his tongue. Crying out her release, her husband gave no mercy as he continued to lick and tease until she came again, screaming his name.

A satisfied look on his face, Colin slid up her body and into her with one hard thrust, filling and stretching her to accommodate his width. "Happy now—" he broke off when she lifted her hips, clenching around him.

Pulling him close, Emily captured his lips. Nibbling down his jaw and neck.

"What were you saying, dear?" she teased.

Colin rolled the two of them over, keeping them joined so she was straddling him. Arching her back, her husband reached up, cupping her breasts, running his hands down her body, sending delicious chills everywhere he touched. Lifting herself up, Emily brought him deeper inside her, gratified to hear his gasp of pleasure. As she rode him, she could feel the combined beating of their heart. Colin looked up at her.

"I love you, lass. Forever and a day."

A silver light filled the room as they came together in release. She collapsed onto his chest. Colin stroked her hair and back, whispering endearments.

"And I love you." Kissing the scar above his eyebrow, she

thanked Terya for blessing her with the one person in the entire world for her and her alone.

Colin manifested blankets over them and held her close. She felt cherished, safe, and well loved.

Emily woke to hear him whisper against her neck.

"Let's stay here forever. Never leave this room."

She groaned, not wanting to move. "We could...but the children would cry when they woke up and saw Santa passed them by." With a yawn, she sat up. They dressed, laughing and smiling and carried the presents out to the tree. It was almost Christmas.

Some of the children fell asleep on the ride home, bellies full and warm in the modified bus. The staff met them on the steps to help carry the little kids to bed.

Maggie gathered the older kids in the library; they were too excited to sleep. Once each had a glass of milk or water, she sat down in the middle of them to read a bedtime story.

Nearing the end, she saw many struggling to stay awake. Hiding yawns behind their hands. "The end. Everyone ready for bed?"

Protests of "we're not tired" and "just a few more minutes" met her ears.

"The sooner you sleep, the sooner Santa will come. Off to bed with you."

They filed up the stairs and climbed into beds as she went to each one, tucking them in. Maggie met Robert in a secret room that opened off of her solar. They'd filled it with the presents from Santa. The staff was waiting to help with the final assembly.

Robert stood back surveying. "It looks like we've bought out every store in the United Kingdom."

Maggie laughed. "They deserve an over-the-top Christmas. Especially after what some of them have been through."

He hugged her. "How are we coming on the animal front? Do I need to rename our home Gwrych zoo?"

His steward chuckled. "We've quite the assortment. Come have a look."

"Wait until you see the giraffe." Maggie grinned, buttoning up her coat.

Quietly so as not to alert any of the children still awake, they went outside, bundled into an SUV and drove the short distance to the barn and outbuildings.

Covering her mouth so as not to burst out laughing at her husband's expression, Maggie coughed into the sleeve of her coat. He turned a mock scowl on her. She held up her hands. "Nothing. Well, the look on your face is kind of funny."

There were the usual cats, dogs, hamsters, and bunnies. Sheep, goats, cows, horses, chickens, and pigs all enjoying the comforts of their new warm home. But the trumpeting is what had him scowling. Taking him by the hand, Maggie led the way to the first of four buildings.

Inside were two elephants. One tiny and one, well, elephant-sized.

"Elephants. The gods save us. I don't want to know what it's going to cost to heat the buildings and the food, no, don't tell me." Robert's steward tried to look serious.

"We have the produce to supply. I've made inquiries into acquiring adjacent land so the animals have room to roam. And we could always sell one of the Picasso's or Dali's if times become desperate."

Robert's horrified look at selling one of his precious paintings had Maggie clapping her hand over her mouth to keep from busting out laughing.

"Ruined. I'll have to go back to pirating. I didn't see Mary, Joseph, and Baby Jesus hiding in one of the stalls. Did I miss them?"

Throwing his hands up, Robert stalked to the next building. It was only going to get worse. The second building contained zebras and camels.

Grumbling under his breath, she thought she caught "getting soft" and "didn't anyone listen when I said normal animals only," but she chose to ignore it.

"You know he's only teasing you about the paintings. I know how much you love beautiful art. Isn't that why we have rooms full of treasure?"

Robert stopped and turned a mock scowl on her. "Asking a pirate to choose between gold and art is like asking you to make a decision between fruit and books." He leaned down, kissing her before he raised an eyebrow. "Aye, we've plenty of gold. Just don't tell anybody I'll happily part with a great deal of it to keep the little monsters happy." Her husband glared at his estate manager. "That goes for you too. Keep quiet about this. I have a reputation to uphold."

"Of course, m'lord."

The man bowed and Maggie giggled, seeing his shoulders shake in silent laughter.

"What's so blasted funny?" Robert grumbled.

"Nothing, love. Come see the rest."

The third and fourth buildings housed big cats. Some were very young. All the animals here were unwanted. The zoos had lost funding and no one had the money to visit so they were in desperate need to find homes for the animals. The animals were purchased from five different zoos, they'd paid a small fortune to get them here in time for Christmas. Maggie had Robert's estate manager tell the zoos to call if they couldn't place others. None of them wanted the animals going to unsavory characters or worse, sold on the black market.

"We need to hire a vet and caretakers."

"Already in progress," The steward answered shooting Maggie an amused look.

She knew Robert liked the chaos of the children and the

animals. But he also liked to grumble. She couldn't wait until he opened her present.

Back in the SUV, Robert rested his head on the steering wheel. He let out a sigh. "Has anyone told Fury and Draken not to eat the animals?"

His manager answered. "Aye. They know. Thought it rather humorous to have a zoo at Gwrych. Said they'd only eat the animals if they became unruly."

"That's all I need, one of the little kids seeing Draken chomp down on their favorite elephant."

Back inside, Maggie hugged him tight, kissing him on the cheek. "You are a big softie and I love you for it."

"The Bengal tiger is rather impressive. Just tell me I won't find the three wise men hanging around trying to steal the rest of my fortune."

Laughing, they went up to bed.

❧ 19 ❧

After putting together the bikes and other large toys, setting them under and around the tree, Colin and Emily were in their bedchamber getting ready for bed.

"Emily, lass. Whatever is the matter? You've been acting strange the past few days." Colin looked at his wife. She was keeping something from him. Holding back. Even earlier when she'd ravished him, he could tell her mind was elsewhere. Dinner was a wonderful affair. Everyone had a good time. Nothing was burnt so what was it?

Removing his boots, Colin placed daggers from each boot on the bedside table. Old habits died hard.

Emily stepped out of the bathroom. By the gods, he wanted to throw her on the bed and ravish her again. "You are stunning. Tonight was perfect, and I mean to have you all to myself for the next few hours. We don't need to sleep." He leered at her, bending her back, tasting.

She broke the kiss. "I...now, don't be angry with me..."

A feeling of dread filled him. The way she was acting, something was very wrong. "What happened?"

"Losing my parents made me realize how important family is. Other than Matt, I have no one left in this world—"

"Emily, I am your family. The twins are your family. And everyone here at Ravensmore and the other Shadow Walkers are your family. I know you miss your parents and your brother, but I'm here for you. We all are." He settled her on his lap in the chair next to the fire, stroking her hair. Watching the fire pick up the gold highlights and turn her red silk robe a deep scarlet.

Troubled gray eyes looked into his. "Oh, Colin. I know how blessed I am. And I have a lovely family but there is one thing missing."

Colin looked at her, confusion and wariness etched across his face. His wife was pale, she had a hand on her stomach as if she might be sick and her heart was beating fast.

"Darlin' you're trembling. Whatever it is, we can fix it."

He knew she heard the strain in his voice. But bloody hell, she was making him as nervous as when she'd given birth to their babes.

She took a deep breath. "I hope you can understand why I did what I did. I want everything out in the open, I should have told you as soon as it happened."

Now he was the one ready to be sick. By the gods, had his wife betrayed him? His muscles clenched and vision narrowed to a small tunnel. "Tell me."

"I know everything that happened with your brother was so terrible. What he did to your family. To you—yet he is your only brother. People can change. Everyone deserves a second chance. Might you make amends?"

His gaze sharpened. "Amends? With a miserable boy long dead?" She was silent. Too silent. "Emily. Tell. Me. What. Happened." The guilt spread across her face, and his insides boiled with worry.

"Don't be mad... You see, I took the twins out in the sleigh, and I somehow ended up at Castle Gloom. I thought you'd started restoring the place. And then...well...I saw you. Only it wasn't you—"

It couldn't be. Clenching his jaw so hard he thought his teeth would crack, he counted to ten in his head, then did it again. Blowing out a breath, he asked, "Who *exactly* was it?"

"It was Hamish... He looked so much like you. But when I looked closer I realized it wasn't you and I was so shocked." She waved a hand in front of her face. "He told me Thorne made him one of you." At his look, she held up a finger. "With losing everyone, I didn't think how angry you might be, I only thought of having *all* of our family together. So I invited him to spend Christmas Eve dinner with us. He never showed up."

Colin barely contained the explosion within. She didn't know how treacherous Hamish could be. The things he might do. Bloody hell. What the fuck was Thorne thinking?

Raising an eyebrow he knocked back a glass of whisky in one gulp, refilled it, and did the same. Anger burned through him. At Emily for not telling him. At Thorne for fucking around with Colin's life. And at his brethren. For surely they had heard or seen Hamish and not told him. The third time he drained the glass he thought he could speak without taking her head off.

"I understand why you did it though you have no bloody idea the kind of man Hamish was—is. When I think of you alone with him... He may be a Shadow Walker but that doesn't mean he's on my side. I mean to have a discussion with Thorne and find out what the devil he's playing at."

"I know you're angry. I'm sorry I waited to tell you..." Her voice trailed off. Colin paced the room like some kind of caged beast. Where was a pack of Day Walkers when he needed them? A nice bloody fight would help him release the rage coursing through his veins. He kept telling himself, *it's not her fault, she didn't know what she was doing.*

His voice harsh, he gritted out, "In the morning, after the kids have opened their presents and we've had brunch, I'll go and speak with my brother. But hear me well. I don't want you anywhere near him until I've spoken with him. This is not up for negotiation."

"Fine." She scowled and climbed into bed, turning her back to him as he stood staring into the fire.

He swore softly. Hamish was back.

PHŒNIX SHADOW

June. He scowled and climbed into the landing bay back
to his life, an odd longing unto the fire.
with Sophie and the Hamishes, as he...

H amish woke alone on Christmas morning. He'd been
back a year, and while Shadow Walkers didn't need to
sleep, it made them feel human. Kept their humanity
intact. Though maybe he should cut the damned thread and
become the asshole everyone thought he was. Frustrated, he
materialized clothing and found himself staring up at the unfinished towers of Castle Gloom.

At least being alone was better than being ignored. Manifesting a bottle of wine, he drank deeply, praying to the gods he
could get drunk. Maybe with enough wine he could numb the
feelings of his past. Why couldn't Thorne have removed the
memories? Let him start anew? Hamish asked, but Thorne
refused without explanation. The jerk.

Hamish hated the holidays, especially bloody Christmas. The
memory flooded his brain before he could push it back. That
was the year he'd turned eight. Colin was thirteen.

Hamish remembered running down the stairs on Christmas
morning. Before he got to the great hall, he heard his father
talking to Colin. Stopping at his father's study, he looked in and
froze. Standing there like a fish out of water, mouth hanging
open, gasping for air. His father who was never one to show

affection reached out and pulled Colin into a bone-crushing hug.

"Ye have shown me what a fine Campbell man ye've become. No longer a boy—a man. I'm so verra proud of you." Their father stopped, suspiciously sniffing.

What the hell? Hamish kept out of sight desperate to find out what was happening to make his father so emotional. Then the man who'd raised him sighed. "I only wish your worthless brother could be like you. If the two of you didn't look so much alike I would swear he wasn't mine. Though your mother says he is as much as it pains her the way the boy's turned out."

Colin agreed. "He only wants to dig in the dirt, ride his horse, and terrorize the staff. Maybe he'll grow up in time, Father."

Their father snorted. "Not bloody likely. I had a cousin just like Hamish. Never came to any good. Ended up drowning in the loch when his boat capsized. He was too drunk to swim to shore. No, Colin. He's a lost cause. Doesn't live up to the Campbell name."

Hamish sunk to his knees on the cold stone floor. He felt as if he'd been kicked in the gut by his horse. How could his father despise him so much when all Hamish ever wanted was his father's approval?

His father spoke again. "'Tis time for you to have this." He slid the ancient ring bearing the Campbell family crest off his finger and placed it in Colin's hand. The heavy gold glinted in the light.

"I am honored, Father." Colin slid the ring on his right hand. Of course it fit perfectly. Colin's smile lit up his face until it looked like the daylight penetrated the very castle walls, throwing the room into stark reality.

Their father looked away to brush something from his eye. A tear?! Hamish had never seen his father shed a tear over anything. Catching sight of Hamish crouched into a ball on the floor staring up at the tableau in front of him, his father looked right through him. The man he called father turned his back on Hamish and led Colin over to the fire, pouring him a glass of whisky, toasting his favorite son.

Hatred filled Hamish. As long as he could remember, he'd wanted the family ring and everything that went with it. Wanted to belong. Now his perfect brother wore the ring, and one day his son would wear it. Hamish would never be a part of the family.

A gull screaming in the distance sent the memory back to the dark recesses of his mind, and Hamish looked down at that very ring...now on his hand. His fist clenched tight at the thought of Colin wearing the ring again.

Full of guilt, he dematerialized to Ravensmore. His brother still thought he was worthless. Wanted nothing to do with him.

Fine. He'd leave a calling card so Colin would know he'd visited. There in the old garrison now converted to a garage were all of Colin's precious toys. Hamish wandered through the large open room, stopping to admire the various machines. His eye caught on a black Aston Martin. Colin's favorite from what he'd heard. He could destroy the entire collection but that might be a bit much.

No, he'd simply make a point of letting his brother know he was back. Blackness filling his heart, Hamish pulled out his dagger and slammed it down. Metal screeched as he buried the blade up to the hilt in the middle of the hood of Colin's favorite car.

❦ 21 ❧

Christmas morning at Gwrych. The first one in a long time. Robert woke to the sound of excited shrieks and shrill voices. Grinning, he kissed Maggie. "Merry Christmas, darlin'. Sounds like the little monsters have discovered the presents Santa brought."

She mumbled something incoherent and rolled over, clutching the pillow to her head. He jumped out of bed and flung the curtains open. Weak sunlight shone in. Outside the world turned to a winter wonderland as the sun hit the snow and ice on the branches turning everything to crystal. Laughing at his wife burrowing into the blankets, he showered and dressed before throwing the covers back and scooping her into his arms.

"Darlin', we better get downstairs before the natives grow restless." She smiled, taking his breath away. Stretching and yawning, she kissed him.

"Merry Christmas to you, husband. Would you like your gift now or later?" He leered at her and she playfully smacked his shoulder. In a prim voice she responded, "Not *that*. That gift is for later this afternoon when the kids are worn out and asleep from all the commotion."

She slid off his lap, her black silk nightgown hugging every curve. "But as punishment for waking me up, you'll have to wait until I'm showered and dressed."

Laughing as he swatted her bottom, she ran for the safety of the bathroom. Knowing he had time, Robert went to the wardrobe and dug into the back corner for his gift to Maggie. Emerging from the bathroom, she wore jeans and a thick wool sweater in an ivory color that set off the red of her hair. Leading her to the chair, he handed her a small box. Her eyes lit up as she opened it. Pulling a picture from the box, a quizzical look crossed her face.

"The design around my name is beautiful. Is it a piece of art?"

Yanking his shirt over his head, he turned enjoying her gasp. Above his left nipple the design stood out in stark contrast, the black ink against the lightly tanned skin. The intricate scrolls, vines and flowers wove around her name.

"How did you hide it? You had my name tattooed on your chest. But will it stay? I thought you couldn't do that?"

"Thorne helped. Yes, it's permanent. Do you like it?" He wanted to swear. Sounding like a schoolboy asking for praise on his homework.

Maggie traced the design. "It's beautiful. I'm honored." She kissed him, twining her fingers in his hair.

"You have marked my soul. I wanted my body to reflect how I feel." He pulled her tight, kissing her, bending her back, wanting to hold her close forever.

"Would you like your present?"

He nodded. Couldn't remember the last time anyone had given him a present. Leaning forward in the chair, he watched as she went to the chest at the foot of the bed, opened it and dug deep. She came up with a cylinder wrapped in festive paper. Opening it, he popped the lid off the cardboard tube and dumped the canvas out. Unrolling it, he leapt to his feet gasping. "The Monet. However did you find it?"

Giggling, she sat in his lap and hugged him. "I called your collector friend, Mr. Goldstein. He was thrilled to help." Seeing his look, she continued. "Well, I have all this gold so I thought you'd like the painting. You do like it, don't you?"

"It's almost as beautiful and breathtaking as you. Growing up poor, I never owned anything of beauty. Once I could afford it, I surrounded myself with beauty. Fine furnishings and homes. Sculpture and paintings. You know, back in the day I met Claude."

Now it was Maggie's turn to gasp. "You met Monet? Tell me."

Robert chuckled. "I was in Paris on business when I came across three Day Walkers cornering a man in an alley. I dispatched them and the man introduced himself as a painter. Claude Monet. It was 1888 if I remember correctly. We became friends, and on a visit he gave me the painting. He said the morning he painted it, he was looking out at the sea and it reminded him of me. I was touched. I'd never held anything so wonderful, created just for me and mine alone. On the way back to Wales, I was attacked by Solien and two Day Walkers. I escaped but lost the painting. I thought it was lost forever. Until you found it."

Maggie pulled her sweater over her head wanting to show him how much she loved him. Standing on tiptoe, she brushed his mouth with hers. "I think the kids can wait a bit longer."

His emotions mixed with the sensation of her body against his had him trembling with need for this amazing woman. He flashed their clothes off, picking her up as she wrapped her legs around his waist. And when she trailed a hand down to trace her name branded on his chest, his soul caught fire.

"I need to feel you inside me." Reaching between them to cup him she leaned back against the wall as the firelight danced across her breasts.

She was his. Needing to possess her, Robert started by kissing her, devouring her mouth and leaning his head down to taste her neck and breasts while she stroked him. With one arm wrapped around her waist supporting her, the other found her center, rubbing, as she clenched around his fingers. He increased the rhythm feeling her tense as she threw her head back in joy letting pleasure take her. Before she could rest, he lifted and impaled her on his hard cock and began thrusting.

"It seems I waited for you a thousand years, my love," he whispered against her neck. Thank the fates for bringing them together.

"Together always. I couldn't go on without you. I love you," she whispered, biting his shoulder.

They came together in ecstasy and sunk down in front of the fire, spent and happy. They lay in each other's arms talking until a knock sounded on the door. A muffled voice called out.

"M'lord, M'lady. The natives are growing restless. I'm afraid they won't hold much longer."

Robert chuckled. "Aye. We'll be down in a moment."

"I guess it's time. Anyway, I'm starved." Maggie licked his neck.

"Start that, darlin', and we'll never make it downstairs." Clearing his throat, he materialized clothing on them. It was quicker and he could hear the noise level increasing. Picking his wife up, Robert dematerialized down to the chaos already in progress.

Everyone rushed them talking at once as they entered the great hall. Robert inhaled deeply, the fresh evergreen and cocoa scents filling his body. Maggie hugged children and tugged him over to the tree. Kids exclaimed over their gifts and Draken popped his head in.

"The wee monsters were awake at five this morning. Fury and I took them out to see the new animal additions Santa brought. I heard a number of them making lists for their birthday." He snorted, a small puff of smoke escaping.

"Draken, did you give the children gold toys?" Robert peered at a small boat a boy with carrot-colored hair was waving in the air.

"Made them myself. Everyone needs their own bit o'gold, wouldn't you say, pirate?"

Robert threw back his head and roared with laughter. Maggie exclaimed over the gifts the children made for her. The cook called everyone in to brunch. "You lot can fix your plate in the dining room then bring it back here to the hall."

He wanted to remember this moment for the rest of his immortal life. Gathered around were his newfound family, together and laughing. Placing a hand over his heart, Robert thanked the gods for bringing them together.

Back at Ravensmore, Emily entered the bedroom, fresh from the shower, toweling her hair dry and faced Colin. "I'm sorry about last night. I can see your point of view."

Eyebrows shot up to his hairline. It was apology enough. "'Tis alright. I will talk to the bloody wanker, make sure he knows his place. But Emily—I doona trust him and willna let him near Ravensmore."

Softening the sting, he hugged her tight. "Merry Christmas, lass." Kissing her, she tasted of toothpaste and smelled like coconut from her shower. "Tropical day today?"

She blushed. "I was in the mood for a warm day so I picked the coconut delight."

"What say we let the kids go ahead without us and I nibble your coconut delight?" He leered at her. Emily smacked his arm.

"As tempting as the offer is, I want to see them open their presents. Bet I can dematerialize downstairs faster than you, husband."

With that she vanished. Colin called after her as he disappeared, "Cheater. You're supposed to count to three."

The great hall looked like every toy store in the United

Kingdom and Europe sent their entire inventory to the castle. The twins were in a large rocking bassinet watching the proceeding with huge, round eyes.

Colin patted them both as he greeted everyone. "Looks like all of ye were mighty good this year. Are you sure Santa didn't leave too much?"

A chorus of "no, we've been really good" answered him.

Brunch was set up in the great hall while Christmas carols played. "Silent Night" filled the air.

As the kids screamed in pleasure over the gifts, he caught Emily watching him. She handed him a small box. "Merry Christmas, sweetie."

Tearing open the paper, he lifted the lid and found a key nestled within. Taking his hand, she handed him his coat, slipped into hers and half-dragged him outside in the lightly falling snow. "It looks like the faeries dusted everything with spun sugar and glass. Isn't it beautiful?" Emily spun in a circle, laughing.

His heart overflowed with love, watching his fierce wife.

Coming to the garage, Emily flipped on the light switch. There sat a Koenigsegg Agera in gunmetal gray. It was rumored to have a top speed of 439 kilometers per hour. What a sweet ride. He couldn't wait to try it out.

"I know I shouldn't have spent so much, but you've been wanting one for months."

Stopping her with a bone-crushing hug, he kissed her until she was breathless. "Are you kidding? It's the best present ever. Once the roads are clear, we're taking her out to see what she can do." Opening the door, he pulled her into the interior and proceeded to thank his wife properly.

Emily lay in his arms dozing while thoughts of Hamish and his parents filled his mind. Colin glanced down at his hands, wedding ring on one hand and the other bare. The Campbell family ring—missing. He remembered Hamish's naked envy when Colin received the ring, his hurt when their father looked right through his younger son. Colin was so excited to get the ring and all it entailed; he didn't stop to think how deeply his brother hurt.

What was family history? Every family member would tell a different truth to events as they recalled them. Could he be wrong about Hamish? Was the truth of the past in Hamish's mind enough to have justified him murdering his own brother?

At a loss, he ran his hands through Emily's hair, stroking the skin along her collarbone. She woke smiling.

Later with a longing glance back at the performance machine, he wondered. Should he try and mend things with Hamish for her? Could he try again with his brother? Shaking his head at the absurdity of the questions, he thought he must be going soft. Deciding he'd deal with it when he came face to face with his younger sibling. After all, looked like Hamish was one of them. He would have thought his brother to be a Day Walker, but truth be told he didn't think Hamish had enough strength of will to have called out to either side for vengeance. What game was Thorne playing?

Leaving the garage, his gaze landed on his baby parked in the corner, well away from the other vehicles. Something wasn't right. Approaching the Aston Martin, Colin blanched. "Bloody fucking hell!"

"What's wrong?" Emily ran over to him, buttoning up her coat.

There in the center of the hood was a dagger buried up to the hilt in the metal. Jaw clenched, Colin cursed. "This is what I get for even considering hearing what Hamish has to say? The bloody arrogant arsehole ruins my baby?" Colin paced across the garage.

"Are you sure it was Hamish?" Emily hung back. Clearly knowing it was wise to give him room.

"It's his all right. I was there when he found it." Colin punched the wall. Plaster rained down on the stone floor as he cursed in a few more languages.

"I'll be back in a bit, lass. I can't let this go unanswered."

Ripping the dagger from the beautiful machine a horrible grating noise filled the air as the car let go of the blade.

"Colin?"

He looked at his wife.

"He is your brother, don't kill him." A nervous laugh escaped as if she wasn't sure if he'd do it or not.

Colin didn't know what he'd do when he laid eyes on the man who murdered him. He kissed Emily and focused on Castle Gloom, his brother's estate. Materializing in the courtyard, shock filled him. A great deal of work had taken place. A few months' worth if he was any judge of the masonry work. How many crews was he employing?

"Enjoying the view?"

That voice. In an instant he was back in the dungeons of Edinburgh Castle reliving his last day as a mortal before Hamish murdered him.

The hell if he'd forgive and forget.

The muscles in his neck tightened. Clenching his jaw, he turned, squared his shoulders, kept his face blank and came face to face with—his brother.

His murderer.

The dagger landed in the unfinished stone wall an inch from Hamish's head. "Hamish. Got your present. Thought I'd return it. 'Tis been a verra long time." Back ramrod stiff, he fought to keep his fingers from blasting his brother with an energy bolt or three.

Prying the embedded dagger from the stone, Hamish wiped it off and slid it into his boot. "Least I could do seeing the shape of my home. Gloom was in ruins when I returned yet Ravensmore still stands. I wonder—what does that say?" Hamish narrowed his eyes and stood in front of Colin.

To Colin it was like looking at a younger version of himself. Though there was a permanent ugly sneer etched on Hamish's face, the corners of his mouth forever turned down.

"Why are you here?"

Hamish laughed. "That's a fine question, isn't it?"

He was wearing charcoal gray pants, a lavender silk shirt, gray leather gloves, and gray suede boots. Truth be told, he looked a bit ridiculous standing there amongst the construction. Gods love him, Hamish had always been a clotheshorse. Colin stared at his betrayer until Hamish spoke again.

"Haven't you heard? I work for Thorne. I'm like you now. Well, in a manner of speaking."

"*You* are *nothing* like me. Stay away from what's mine. Bother Emily again and I'll destroy you, Thorne be damned." Growling the words at Hamish, Colin couldn't speak to him, couldn't look at him one more blasted second without punching the arrogant smile right off his face.

Dematerializing back to Ravensmore, Colin heard Hamish's mocking laughter, carried on the wind.

"See you soon, *brother mine*."

THANK YOU SO MUCH FOR READING! I HOPE YOU ENJOYED Iced in Shadow. Next up is, Reborn in Shadow, where there's always two sides to every story. I hope you love it.

IF YOU'D LIKE TO RECEIVE AN EMAIL ABOUT MY UPCOMING new releases, please join my mailing list. Visit my website, cynthialuhrs.com

ABOUT THE AUTHOR

Cynthia Luhrs spends her time out on the deck, looking into the woods, imagining what if. She writes women's fiction, time travel romance, contemporary romance, family sagas, paranormal romance, and thrillers. Readers say her books (well not the thrillers, those are gritty) are light-hearted reads to escape reality.

She lives in the mountains of North Carolina with two rescued tiger cats, has always been a reader, and is overly fond of sparkly flip flops and pretty pens. Though now that she lives in the mountains she's going to have to find fabulous boots, mittens, and hats!

Keep up with her on her website

facebook.com/cynthialuhrsauthor

instagram.com/cynthialuhrs

bookbub.com/authors/cynthia-luhrs

goodreads.com/cynthialuhrsauthor

www.ingramcontent.com/pod-product-compliance
Lightning Source LLC
Chambersburg PA
CBHW012237190626
46810CB00021B/3442